PCH

Listed

A PORT CITY HIGH NOVEL

SHANNON FREEMAN

SADDLEBACK
EDUCATIONAL PUBLISHING

High School High

Taken

Deported

The Public Eye

The Accident

Listed

Traumatized

A Port in Pieces

SADDLEBACK
EDUCATIONAL PUBLISHING
www.sdlback.com

ISBN-13: 978-1-62250-773-3
ISBN-10: 1-62250-773-8
eBook: 978-1-61247-984-2

Printed in Guangzhou, China
NOR/1014/CA21401594

19 18 17 16 15   1 2 3 4 5

ACKNOWLEDGMENTS

Thank you, Saddleback! This relationship has changed my world, my family, and the core of who I am. Your belief in me as a writer made me believe in myself even more. Arianne McHugh, you made my dreams a reality. I never thought that I would be where I am right now in this journey. You hit the fast forward button in my life. For that, I am eternally grateful.

Carol Pizer, you tell me "no" when I want to hear "yes." You make me stretch until I find the perfect storyline. The process that we go through together makes for a better work of fiction and has made me a better writer. I can't imagine this journey without you.

I would like to give a special thank you to Evette Rodgers. You always show up to work my book signings, even after a long day of work. Not only do you give to me, but you give to our students and our community alike. It seems that your pot never runs dry. Thank you for always being willing.

Thank you to my students and the teenagers in our community, who just keep coming back, eager for more Port City High. I love it! You make writing fun. I love our discussions and book talks, even though sometimes you are not pleased with the direction of the story. I love your brutal honesty. Keep the feedback coming!

I could not do any of this without my family. You are my support system and my reason. You make it easy to keep working when other people are resting. For my husband, I don't know where I would be without you. Those aren't just empty words—that's the truth. Derrick Freeman, you gave my life purpose. You loved me before I loved me, and that made me who I am today. For that, I will love you until the end of time.

Prologue

As Shane stared out of the plane's window, she basked in the thrill of a new experience. This trip was a pleasant surprise, one that Brandi had also been included in. The girls were accompanying Marisa on her journey to Los Angeles, California, for a meet and greet with the plastic surgeon who was going to remove the scarring from her face. In the fall there had been a dreadful car accident. A freshman twirler was killed, and Marisa had been thrown into a windshield.

Shane looked over at her two best friends. The girls were using Brandi's tablet and gossiping about their new relationships, which had started over Christmas break. Friender was the best way to catch up on all gossip during the holidays. They were so focused on Port City that they were missing the plane's landing in Los Angeles.

"Hey, put that thing away. We're touching down!" She faked a scream by opening her mouth wide, and she grabbed her two best friends. There was so much she wanted to see and do in Los Angeles.

"Shane, you have to see the girl Mattie's dating now. The boy has no standards. I can't believe I dated him for all those years," Brandi said, shaking her head.

"Really, B? We are landing in Los Angeles, baby. I want to hear nothing about those little kiddy relationships. I want to go to the Santa Monica Pier, Venice Beach, the Walk of Fame, eat good sushi, get a spray tan, get waxed, and shop till I drop. That's all I can think about."

"Girl, that's enough." Brandi laughed at her friend's excitement. Shane's enthusiasm was contagious. Brandi looked out as the plane landed.

"Shopping!" Marisa almost yelled. "I'm so happy you came with me. What's a trip to L.A. without my girls? I need moral support. I'm kind of nervous. I've done photo shoots before, but my self-esteem was a lot better then. With my face still scarred, I feel ugly, ya know? I want to hide, and they want me to wear my scars with pride. It's nerve-racking."

"Ugly? You are so far from ugly," Shane scolded.

"You aren't even in the same zip code with ugly," Brandi said, showing them her tablet. "Now this is ugly. Woof." There was a picture of Matthew's new girlfriend. They all laughed.

Once the airplane parked at the gate,

the girls gathered their personal items and left, saying good-bye to the flight attendants as they walked toward the jetway. They were finally in Los Angeles!

"*Niñas*, be careful and stay together at all times," Mrs. Maldonado told them. She had accompanied them on the trip, even though they insisted they didn't need a chaperone. "No. You are crazy if you think you're ready to go Los Angeles alone. It's a huge city! I don't even know if *I'm* ready for it," Mrs. Maldonado had told them.

Near baggage claim, they were greeted by their limo driver. He was holding a sign that read Maldonado.

"I think that's for us," Brandi told them.

"What tipped you off, genius?" Shane asked.

"Don't be snarky. Chill out," Marisa scolded Shane.

The limo driver helped them with their luggage, and they loaded up to take the ride to the Beverly Hills Hotel. That's where Sculptique of Beverly Hills had them staying.

"Everything is so different here," Shane said, in awe of the drive.

Each of them stayed glued to the limo's windows as they watched the California scenery. Once they were in Beverly Hills, the view became more residential. The homes that lined the streets looked much different than the brick homes in Texas. The mega-mansions they could see looked to be Tuscan or Spanish. The yards were neatly manicured. Cool-weather flowers—English primroses, pansies, and Iceland poppies—were in bloom. The more expensive homes were tucked away behind gates. And the most expensive were up in the hills, on narrow canyon roads.

Even though it was December, Mother Nature had not been notified. It looked like a beautiful spring day, with people out jogging, walking their dogs, doing yoga, and dining alfresco.

"I'm never leaving," Shane said as she got lost in the whole scene. When they arrived at the hotel, they were greeted by the scent of roses instead of the smells of the Port City refineries. They were worlds away from home, and it was eye-opening.

When they got to their suite, they unpacked and soaked in the luxury.

"This is like living in a dream," Marisa said, lying on the bed. "I thought my modeling career was over. I finally see what *abuelita* means when she says, 'When life gives you lemons, make *limonada*.' I just wish that Bethany could see this too. She would have loved it."

"I have a feeling Bethany is seeing L.A. with us," Shane said.

Marisa nodded in agreement. If it hadn't been for Bethany's mom, Marisa would still be in a dark place. She had fallen into a deep depression following the accident. She blamed herself for her young friend's death. The new advertising campaign for the plastic surgeon had given Marisa a new lease on life. She knew she had to mourn and move one. She had to live her life. Somewhere, there was a balance between grief and happiness.

"Now, let's get out of here. We are too close to Rodeo Drive to be locked up in this hotel," Shane told them.

They changed their clothes and hit the streets of Beverly Hills. When they arrived on Rodeo Drive, it was much more expensive than they had imagined.

"A thousand dollar tank top? I'm taking a picture of that," Brandi said, pulling her phone out.

"Girl, stop looking country," Shane said, making her put the phone away.

Brandi went back and snapped the picture anyway and sent it straight to Friender. The attention she got on the Internet let her know she wasn't the only one appalled by the pricey items in the Beverly Hills shops.

Luckily, they located a boutique that was in their price range. Kind of. They splurged and bought spring clothes that were sure to be a hit at home. As they dined outside at one of the restaurants, they started chatting with their server. She seemed to know everything about Los Angeles.

Their server told them to go to Santee Alley to do some real shopping. She told them about the best sushi spots in L.A. Shane was adamant about getting real sushi while she was in California. She heard that the Westside had some of the best sushi outside of Japan, and she was determined to eat her way through the town's *omakase*. There was even a New Year's Eve party on the Santa Monica Pier that their server said not to miss. They wanted to see it all before returning to ho-hum Port City.

Marisa had to report for work early the next morning. So after they did some more shopping, they decided to eat dinner and rent a movie.

At five thirty the next morning, a car picked them up and delivered them to Marisa's set. The cold California air chilled them to the bone. Shane and Brandi had never gone with Marisa to work. They were usually at school, so this was special.

When they arrived, Marisa went straight to hair and makeup, where the professionals worked their magic. They made Marisa look beautifully natural. They needed the scars to be visible, but they still wanted her beauty to shine. The shoot was one of the easiest Marisa had ever done.

The plastic surgeon, Dr. Neimann, took to her immediately. Marisa's story had struck a chord in him. He had lost his own daughter to a drunk driver when she was a teenager. When Marisa's agent called him for his opinion about the facial scars, he knew immediately that he wanted to take on Marisa's case gratis.

The doctor was a modest man with a funny sense of humor. Marisa felt comfortable with him. She felt she could trust him from the moment she was introduced. She was really happy when he made a connection with Brandi and Shane too. He took them out for lunch at his favorite restaurant, the Kosher Kitchen.

Mrs. Maldonado wasn't used to this type of cuisine, especially when their server brought out the "lamb pops." She wrinkled her nose and politely declined, stating that Bambi was not going anywhere near her plate. She was not an adventurous eater. She shied away from trying anything out of the ordinary, but the three girls welcomed everything different. They enjoyed their first kosher meal and all of the history that went along with it.

During lunch, Dr. Neimann explained every treatment Marisa would undergo, but only when she was ready. He wanted her back to her old self by senior year. They had a long road ahead, but he assured her that it would be worth it.

The car returned them to the hotel in time for a nap. Then they prepped for a night on the town. They walked the Venice Beach boardwalk and enjoyed the night-life. It was cold out, but they were bundled up. They met the most interesting people, including a man twirling fire. Marisa was amazed. He did things with his batons that she could only dream of doing. Venice Beach was magical. If only they could bring a small piece of this unique scene back to Port City.

They were up the next morning ready to shop at the legendary Santee Alley, and it was better than they could have imagined. There was something for everyone. They bought souvenirs for their families. Shane even snuck in a gift for Coach Rob. He loved watches, and she found one she knew he'd like. He was her weakness. Everything inside of her said she shouldn't be dating her teacher, but something kept drawing her to him. She knew she was in big trouble.

It was New Year's Eve, their last night in Los Angeles. The outfits they purchased at Santee Alley that day were perfect for the party on the Santa Monica Pier.

When they arrived, the area around the pier was chaotic. They purchased party masks from a vendor and went to join the crowd. They saw a large group of kids gathered together on the beach and decided to see if they could join their party. They felt free. It was like no other experience in the world.

As soon as they sat down on one of the many blankets spread out on the sand, one of the guys introduced himself and his other two friends. They talked and laughed, enjoying ringing in the New Year with these complete strangers, who looked totally different from the guys back home.

Within the hour, they were paired

up and cuddling with their new friends, trying to shield themselves from the cold air that blew in from the Pacific Ocean.

"I'm freezing," Brandi shivered. "Y'all cool and all, but I need some heat."

" 'Y'all.' I love Texas girls. Your accent is so cute," Brandi's cuddle partner told her.

"We don't have accents," Brandi retorted.

"Maybe not in Texas, but here in Cali, you have an accent."

"I'm calling for the car," Marisa said, locating her cell phone.

"You have a driver?" her new friend asked. "*Who* are you?"

"Just a Texas girl," Marisa said shyly.

"Well, let us show you some of our town, our way."

Everyone piled into the limo. The boys had the driver going everywhere. They pulled up their Friender pages and went to every party they had VIP passes for. As they walked Hollywood Boulevard, the girls could not believe where they were. By the time they arrived at Shoes, it was almost midnight. They decided to go inside and party in the New Year. When they were allowed through the red ropes, they looked at all of the legendary shoes on display in the shadowboxes along the walkway. They even had a pair of Judy Garland's ruby slippers from *The Wizard of Oz*.

If they could have taken these three boys back home with them, they would have. They seemed perfect for them. Nobody wanted the night to end. The countdown to the New Year brought everyone onto the dance floor. Marisa, Shane, and Brandi raised their soda-filled glasses and gave a loud whoop as they welcomed in the next year.

On cue, their cute tour guides turned to each of them and pecked them on the lips. It was innocent, it was cute, and it was exactly what they wanted. It was the best New Year's the girls had ever had.

CHAPTER 1

Shane

After their trip to Los Angeles, Shane's eyes opened to life's possibilities. When they were freshmen at Port City High, graduation seemed far away. But now, college was only eighteen months off. Soon Shane would be living on a university campus, making decisions for herself. She could almost taste the freedom.

Life after Port City was becoming a reality. The last thing she wanted was to have her high school career have a negative impact on her college options. With that being said, she knew it was time to end things with Coach Rob. She opened her purse and looked at the watch she'd purchased for him during her trip to Los Angeles. It was perfect. She knew he would love it. As she looked at the watch, she knew what it meant. It was her good-bye.

Shane had to let Coach go before it was too late. After all, she was still a virgin and planned to take it with her to college. She couldn't let her friends down. They had a pact. She knew if she continued her relationship with Coach Rob, she would put her plans in jeopardy. Two people could only hold out for so long.

The problem was she loved spending time with him. She was deeply attracted to him. And she'd started sneaking out after her parents were asleep. Sooner or later, she would get caught. She would miss those late-night conversations the most. They had a true connection, one she didn't share with any boy her own age.

Weeks ago at the seawall, they had been listening to music late at night in his parked car. An Aaliyah song came on the radio, "Age Ain't Nut'n but a Number."

"That's you," he said to her. "You remind me of Aaliyah and how she was at your age, mature beyond her years."

She leaned over and kissed him as the water beat against the rocks. She wondered how many star-crossed lovers had done the same over those rocks through the years. If those rocks could speak, what stories would they tell? Before she knew it, he reclined her seat and moved to her side. He began to kiss her. She could feel his body as the intensity of the situation grew. She pulled away from him. "Coach Rob."

"Wait. Don't say it." He kissed her again, more passionately than ever before. She couldn't lose her virginity to a teacher, though. This did not fit her picture of her first time. It was going to be something wonderful, not something shameful. And certainly not in a car. All the car's windows were steamy. The heat from their bodies had made sure of that.

She reached up and touched his face. "I really need to go."

He dropped his head onto her shoulder, trying to compose himself. "I know. I just need a second." He was about to return to the driver's seat when he saw a police car. "Shoot. We have to go. We've got company."

"Company?" Shane turned around to see the flashing red lights. "Daddy knows every cop in Port City. I'm dead."

"Girl, this is more serious than that. Just let me talk."

The cop tapped on the window. "Hey, this seawall is closed. You two are going to have to take it on home," he said, shining the flashlight into the car. "Now move along."

"Yes, sir," Coach Rob said, starting the car immediately.

They sat in silence for the ride back

to Shane's house. They knew they had dodged a bullet. Luckily, the police officer had never really looked at her. If he had, there was no telling what would have happened. When the coach pulled onto Shane's street, he parked a few houses away.

"Shane, I need for you to know something. You are the coolest, funniest, most beautiful person I have ever dated, but we can't keep doing this. It's too dangerous. For both of us."

"What are you saying?"

"I want you to be mine, all mine. That can't happen while you are still in high school."

"Are you ending this?" she asked, feeling heartbroken.

"Yeah, I am." He gently kissed her on the lips.

"I'm not ready. I can't let you go, so please don't expect me to. Dangerous or not, you are more than worth the risk. I'm falling in love with you, and I can't help myself."

He kissed her again, but this time the gentleness was replaced with desperation. He knew she was right. Their connection was too strong.

That L.A. trip had been just what the doctor ordered. She needed a little time away from him in order to clear her head. She felt like she could think clearly again. She ran her hand across the watch that sat in her purse, as if she was touching him. "Good-bye, my love."

She opened the door to his office as she did every day, but today she was a bit taken aback. Ms. Simpson was sitting on top of his desk, wearing a short pencil skirt and walking him through the school's computer system. They looked to be enjoying each other's company. She turned to greet Shane as she entered the office.

"Hi, Shane, did you need something?" Ms. Simpson asked.

"Not from you," Shane snapped, rolling her eyes. From the look on Ms. Simpson's face, she was not expecting that rude reply. "Hey, Coach," Shane said, looking at him as though he had been caught. Ms. Simpson, perhaps noticing the tension in the room, decided she should let him take care of this student. She looked at Coach Rob suspiciously and left the two of them alone.

"What was that?" he scolded Shane when Ms. Simpson was out of earshot.

"What?"

"You can't do that. You have me looking like—"

"Like what? Like somebody in a relationship with a student. I don't care. She was all over you. All over your desk. How am I supposed to feel? Never mind, just take this." She threw the watch at him. "I don't even care anymore. Go be with that old maid if you want to." She had walked all the way to the gym to end their relationship. Now here she was ready to fight for it. She was all over the map. What was her problem?

"You know I don't want her," he said gently, walking over to her. "Come here." He touched her chin to bring her gaze to meet his. "I missed you."

She softened. "I missed you too."

CHAPTER 2

Brandi

*W*hat do you have there, baby girl?" Mrs. Haywood asked her oldest daughter.

"Oh, it's just this flyer I picked up about the debate team. I'm debating trying out," Brandi said, snorting at her dorkiness.

"Debate, huh? That's cool. I think that you would like the debate team. You're always arguing about something anyway. Maybe you should use your powers for good. When are the tryouts?"

"Today. I just don't want to make a fool of myself, though. What if I look dumb?"

"Baby girl, don't ever shy away from a

good challenge. It's the only way you know what you're made of. Just rip the Band-Aid off. Give it a try. What's the worst that can happen?"

"I don't make the team."

"Exactly, and you're not on the team anyhow, so your life won't change, right?"

"Yeah, I guess you're right, Mom. Thanks," she said, kissing her mother and heading upstairs to finish getting ready for school.

"Take an umbrella. It's supposed to rain today," her mother yelled after her.

Brandi stared at her reflection in the mirror. If she was going to get up in front of a group of people, the last thing she wanted was to be unsure about her appearance. She found a white Ralph Lauren uniform shirt and paired it with a pair of khaki skinny jeans, a brown belt, and her Ralph Lauren riding boots. She added a white infinity scarf that complimented the white shirt perfectly. She grabbed her classic peacoat and made it to her bus stop just as the bus pulled up.

The yellow school bus crept through Port City, giving her time to think about the advice her mom had given her. By the time they pulled up to PCH, she had made up her mind. She was trying out for the debate team.

The debate team tryouts were all she could think of all day. She was a bundle of excitement and nerves.

When the debate coach, Mr. McAfee, called her name, she felt as though her heart was in her throat. She went to the stage and pulled a topic out of a jar: childhood obesity. *Okay, this should be easy*, she thought.

The coach gave her one minute to prepare and organize her thoughts. When she started speaking, her nervousness seemed to disappear. The crowd hung on her every word, motivating her. She fed off their attention. She felt at home speaking before this group, until Mr. McAfee started to question her arguments.

"So you believe that it's the child's fault if he or she is obese?"

"No, that's not what I'm saying."

"Yes, that's exactly what you are saying. You said, and I quote, 'Children are obese because they need to exercise more and have a healthier diet.' That tells me that a five year old is responsible for their own weight issues."

"No, I didn't mean five-year-olds, I meant teenagers."

"But that's not what you said. You said children."

At that point, Brandi wanted to run off the stage. She didn't want to defend herself against this mean man posing as a debate coach. She tried to compose herself. "Look," she fired back, "you are twisting my words. Of course parents have to assist their children in decision making when it comes to eating and exercise. But ultimately, parents cannot be around their children all the time. It's up to the child to make some decisions for themselves, and to do that they have to learn self-control at a young age."

"Thank you, Brandi. You can be seated," Mr. McAfee said.

"You did great," one girl told her as she sat down.

"Yeah, right. He ripped into me," she whispered back.

She didn't think she would actually make the debate team, but it had been fun trying out. At least she could say she tried.

The next morning when she arrived at school, she saw one of the other girls who tried out for the team. "Hey, check out the list. It's posted on Mr. McAfee's door," the girl said.

Brandi rushed down the hall. She made the team! She stood there staring at her name.

"I was impressed by your performance yesterday," Mr. McAfee said, startling her.

"Oh, thanks. I thought that I did a terrible job."

"No, most people would have folded under the pressure, but you held your own and came back to your original point. Don't worry. I'll teach you how to work out the bugs. Congratulations," he said, opening the door to his classroom.

Brandi felt as though she was on cloud nine for the rest of the day. For some reason, this new world seemed to be calling her, and she wasn't putting up a fight.

CHAPTER 3

Marisa

*I*t was a horrible idea, Marisa thought, sitting in the auditorium for another audition. Before, she was only nervous about her abilities to make the character believable. But since the accident last semester, she was incredibly self-conscious about her facial scars. She had already started one round of treatments with Dr. Neimann, but that wasn't enough. Her confidence had improved since the accident, but she was not at her best. Not just yet.

She had completed one twirling performance since that deadly accident that killed her friend Bethany, but it had been in Bethany's honor. It was different. Very different. This play was optional. She was using it to challenge herself, and she was beginning to wonder if it was even worth it.

Usually the same school plays were performed year after year, but not this year. The drama teacher, Mrs. Scapin, was a woman of many talents and had actually written her own play. The tryouts gave students a sneak peek into the play's topic. The role Marisa really wanted was pretty dramatic, but so was her life. She decided to read for two parts.

The first role was Tania, a runaway teenager who had lost her mother during a disagreement between rival gangs. The second was the counselor attempting to help this group of lost teenagers. Marisa knew she could really play both these characters. She could relate to the pain Tania

felt when she lost her mother by chan-
neling her grief over the loss of Bethany,
which still overcame her at times. She
could also relate to the counselor because
she had played that role with her friends
on so many occasions. Too many to count.
There always seemed to be drama.

Mrs. Scapin had picked Tania's most
dramatic scene in order to test her actors'
abilities. When Marisa got onstage, her
portrayal of Tania truly dazzled the audience. She just hoped they felt the connection that she felt during her performance.

When all of the actors completed
their auditions, Mrs. Scapin had the dance
teacher, Mrs. Woods, step onstage to talk
to the potential cast members.

"This may come as a bit of a surprise to
y'all," she started to say, "but, Mrs. Scapin
had me choreograph small dance roles for
the monologues. Tomorrow, I need each
of you to meet me here, ready to dance. I

promise it won't be anything too difficult. For the boys, do not worry, we will only do what will make you comfortable."

If Marisa had doubts about this play before, they were now confirmed. She was far from a dancer. After much thought, she decided to opt out of the play. She couldn't see herself dancing without a baton in her hand. She wasn't ready for all the demands of this play.

Shane and Brandi were waiting for her by the auditorium doors when she was done.

"How was it?" Shane asked.

"Was it a good play? I heard Mrs. Scapin wrote it herself," Brandi said.

"I'm not doing it," Marisa told them.

"Why?" they both asked in unison.

"There's a solo dance routine. I'm not trying to do all that. I just want to act, not dance."

"Girl, please! What do you call all that you do on the football field? If you couldn't dance, you definitely couldn't pull off half of your routines."

"B is right, Mari. You can do this."

Marisa thought about her friends' advice. *I guess they're right. I can at least try. Plus, I wanted a challenge.* "Okay, I'll come back tomorrow and see what happens. But please believe this, I won't be too disappointed if I don't get a part."

When Marisa went back to the auditions the next day, Mrs. Woods showed the girls some basic moves. She wanted to test their dancing skills. While they worked out the kinks, she worked with the boys. She had choreographed a surprisingly masculine dance routine for them.

As they practiced, Marisa realized her friends were right. It was easy for her to pick up the routine after countless hours working on twirling performances. She was pleased with the end product. Once they started the dance portion of the auditions, she was actually having fun. It got her even more excited about being part of the play.

After each person had completed their dance moves onstage, the judges gave them a fifteen-minute break. After the break, the roles would be assigned. Then there would be an announcement about rehearsal times. They had a lot of work to do, and Mrs. Scapin had already told them that she wanted to get started as soon as possible.

Marisa went to the restroom and then got a drink at the water fountain, but she still had ten minutes to spare. She decided to step outside and get some fresh air. It was cold out, and her jacket was still in the auditorium. But she didn't care. The forty-degree wind blew through her clothes, chilling her to the bone. She closed her eyes and took in the moment.

When she opened her eyes, there was a white lady and a boy, who looked to be mixed, standing there. "Oh, hi. You startled me," Marisa told them. They seemed an odd pair.

"I'm looking for the front office to enroll my son in school here."

"I'd be happy to show you where it's located. I'm headed that way now."

"Dustin, aren't you going to introduce yourself?" his mother asked.

"I'm Dustin," he responded dryly.

His mother looked aggravated. "What's your name, honey?" she asked Marisa.

"I'm Marisa," she said. When they arrived at the office door, she said. "Well, enjoy your time at PCH, Dustin. Nice to meet you."

She was the last one back in the auditorium after her encounter with Dustin and his mom. Each of the students received an envelope with their part and rehearsal times. When Marisa opened her envelope, she was thrilled. She had gotten the role of Tania. It was what she had wanted all along. She sat staring at the notecard. A lot of the kids were filing out of the auditorium, but Marisa didn't move. She wanted it all to soak in. The play, her role, how much she loved the dance element, and how happy she felt. A small smile crept over her face. Yes! This was a moment of victory. She couldn't wait to share the news with her friends and family.

CHAPTER 4

Cover-Up

By mid-January, a chill seeped into their small town. In other parts of the country, people would love to have Port City's forty-five degree lows. But here, everyone was used to warmer weather. The folks who lived in this part of Texas saw the winter as an inconvenience and wanted spring to come as quickly as possible.

Shane and Marisa decided to stay at Brandi's house, watch movies, and veg out in their Snuggies and oversized slippers. Cold weather was the perfect opportunity to be at home with the people you loved. The girls were determined that this Saturday night would be drama free and filled with food and friends. As they sat around the fireplace roasting marshmallows for the s'mores they were making, they caught up on all of the week's events.

"Congratulations again on landing that part in the play, Mari. You are going to be great. Can I get a sneak peek at the script?" Shane asked her. She was a drama club kid too, but this year she opted out of the play. She wanted to focus more on journalism and learn everything that she could in order to run the newspaper her senior year. She knew she was next in line, and she wanted to be ready.

"Thanks, Shane. And no, you can't see the script. It's top secret. Y'all better be there on opening day. We have a while before the actual performance. It's going to be after state testing is over. You know that's all they focus on at our school. Everything gets planned around testing."

"I'm getting commended in all areas this year," Brandi announced. "I just have to. I need to get into somebody's college, and a good one too."

"I don't know if college is for me. I love to entertain. I want to do that," Marisa admitted to her friends.

"They have colleges that focus on the arts. You need to look into that, Mari. I'm sure you'd be accepted. You're awesome at everything you do," Shane commented, complimenting her friend.

"Girl, you have a way with words," Marisa said, trying to get her marshmallows onto her graham cracker.

"Hey, are you three roasting marshmallows without me?" Raven pouted as she came downstairs after her bath. Marisa immediately handed Raven the s'more she had just made. Raven was ten now and looking more like a tween than the little girl they were all used to. She was still their baby, though.

"RaRa, what's going on in your world?" Shane asked her. She didn't have a little sister. Raven was as close as she was going to get. When Brandi was abducted their freshman year, Shane and Marisa formed an even tighter bond with Raven. She had only been eight at the time, but she put the pieces of Brandi's abduction together and ensured that her sister made it back home.

"Same ol' same. There is somebody who's try'n to holler at me, though."

Shane almost choked on her graham cracker. "Try'n to holler at you? When you start talking like that?"

Raven shrugged her shoulders and the three of them laughed. "You need to hang out with people your own age, li'l mama," Marisa told her. "You not grown."

"I'm going to middle school next year," Raven announced, as if that answered all their questions.

Shane's phone beeped, signaling that she had received a text message. She crossed the family room, tripping over blankets and pillows that were scattered around for their slumber party. When she got to the phone, a huge smile spread across her face as she read the words on her screen. She typed some words into her phone and rejoined her friends in front of the fireplace.

"What?" Brandi asked her.

"What what?" Shane replied.

"That was him, huh?" Marisa asked, narrowing her eyes at her friend.

"Y'all trippin'. I'm getting something to drink. Y'all need anything?"

"I want something," Raven told her.

Shane practically floated out of the room.

"You *want* to go upstairs. We need to talk to Shane. Grab a juice box out of the fridge."

"Bran-di," Raven whined. Brandi gave her sister a look that let her know she had to go away. Raven wasn't happy, but she complied with her sister's wishes.

When Shane returned from the kitchen, a big silly grin was still on her face.

"Girl, you are going to have to come clean 'cause you lookin' guilty. Was that Coach Rob or not?"

"Yeah, dang! Don't look at me like that, Brandi."

"It was supposed to be over, Shane," Marisa told her.

"Yeah, well. I wasn't about to serve him up to Miz Simpson. She be lookin' at him all thirsty like."

"You dumb. Let her have him. He ain't all that anyway."

"Please, he makes my teeth sweat. Now, give me my Snuggie and my pillow. I'm going to bed."

"Good idea," Marisa and Brandi agreed, playing into Shane's plan.

When they fell asleep, Shane crept through the house and out the front door. Coach Rob was there waiting with a cup of hot chocolate. They drove to their favorite spot on the seawall and watched as the ships passed.

"What are we doing, Rob? This is crazy. It's like I'll do anything you ask, no matter what the risk."

He looked at her wrapped up in her blanket, sipping her hot chocolate. "I don't know, Shane. All I know is that I've never felt like this before. If I have to wait for you, I will." He looked deeper into her eyes and began to kiss her. He unwrapped her blanket. "You don't need this," he said. "I'm what you need."

"Rob," she said breathlessly. "I need to get back to Brandi's house. The sun will be up soon."

"A few more minutes," he said, trying to kiss her again. But Shane didn't want to give him a few more minutes. She couldn't bear the thought of breaking a pact with her friends, and she could tell where this was heading.

"No, I really need to go."

It was five o'clock in the morning when she tried to get back into Brandi's house, but the front door was no longer accessible. It had been locked. Shane panicked. *Do they know that I'm gone? How am I supposed to get back in?* Running out of options, she decided it was best to try to wake up Brandi or Marisa.

She tapped on the front window. There was no movement in the house. *These heifers sleeping too hard.* She started to send them a text when a light came on in the living room. *Oh, thank God,* she thought. But then she was face-to-face with Mr. Haywood, who was on his way to work.

"Shane? What are you doing out here?" he asked, confused.

At this point she was freezing. "I was feeling sick, and I needed some air. I locked myself out somehow."

Mr. Haywood didn't look like he was buying her story, but he was in a rush to leave for his job at the refinery, so he let it go. "Okay, Shane. Just get back in the house where it's warm."

She crept back into the family room. She slid back into her sleeping bag, which was between Brandi and Marisa. She tried to absorb some of their body heat. Brandi elbowed her as the cold from Shane's body seeped through her flimsy sleeping bag.

"Shane, why you all up on me?" she asked sleepily.

"Look, girl. I'm freezing. Please let me snuggle."

"You better not have—"

"Go back to sleep, B. I'll tell you later." She lay awake for another thirty minutes, thinking about Coach Rob and the way he made her feel. She was trying to take her v-card with her to college, but this man was making it harder and harder.

CHAPTER 5

Shane

Their journalism class was moving along under the leadership of Whitley Harris. Shane had been upset at the beginning of the year when Whitley got the position of editor in chief instead of her, but she had to admit that Mrs. Monroe had been right about Whitley. It was her time to lead.

Shane's position as managing editor was perfect for her. She was able to take on major responsibilities while still learning her position for next year. Yes, there were always things that she would have done differently if she had been the editor in chief, but she wasn't. She let Whitley run her ship the way she saw fit. And Shane was happy to do whatever Whitley needed.

Shane's dad always told her, "A true leader must first learn how to follow," and that's exactly what she was doing. Shane and Whitley worked well together and met all of their deadlines. Mrs. Monroe was very pleased with the school's paper and even more pleased with the direction of the yearbook.

As they worked on the graphics and layout for the yearbook, there was a knock on the door. Mrs. Monroe was called into the hallway. Mr. Spears, the assistant principal, came into the room to monitor the students while she was outside. He said he loved what they were doing as a class. And he even sat for a new yearbook picture with the journalism team.

When Mrs. Monroe returned, a new student accompanied her. "Class, let me have your attention for a minute, please.

This is Dustin Chaisson. He will be joining our team. I know having someone new to our school included in the newspaper staff is out of the ordinary. But Dustin played a big part in the success of his school newspaper in Louisiana, and we need to get him plugged in quickly. Please, let's make him feel at home. Would you like to say anything, Dustin?"

"Hi, class," he said, gaining a few chuckles. "I just want to jump in and help where I can. Before we moved from Lake Charles, I was very active in journalism. I'm not trying to come and take anybody's job or step on toes. I just want to help and learn whatever I can about the way you guys do things here in Texas. I'm excited and can't wait to get started."

He found a seat at a table where some students had gathered around a computer, planning their layouts.

"Hey, Dustin, I hope you don't think I can see the computer with that big

Afro blocking the screen," Hannah said, reaching out to touch his hair.

"Hey now, that's for looking only, no touchy-touchy," Dustin said, trying to dodge her hand.

"Ooh, it's so soft. You mixed or something?" Hannah asked him.

"Yeah, Mom is white Creole and Dad is black Creole. However you look at it, I'm still Creole."

Shane laughed a bit. She definitely could understand that. She got the same reaction from people who didn't know her well. "What are you? Mixed or something?" She heard it all the time. She liked the way he handled it. She went over to introduce herself.

"Hey, new kid," she said, "welcome to the team. If you need any help getting adjusted, holler at me."

"Sure," he said, looking at her curiously.

"What? I have broccoli in my teeth or something?"

"No, I hope this isn't weird, but you remind me of my sister. I mean ... she's two, but I can see her looking just like you one day. Weird." He pulled out his phone and showed her a picture of a cute little girl who looked every bit as Creole as he did.

"Aw, she's a cutie."

"Yeah, that's Madison. She's my heart. She bad, though."

Shane shared a picture of her nephew with him as well. "This is my nephew, Aiden. That's my little man. He'll be two this summer, so when you say bad ... I know what you mean."

"Cool, maybe we can get them together some time. You can show me Port City."

This caught Shane off guard. She wasn't sure if he was being nice or flirting. She thought about his offer for a second. "Hey, that may be cool. We've never really done a play date."

"Well then, it's a date. No ... not a date. A play date. You know what I mean, right?"

Shane laughed. "It's all good. Well, I have to get back to work. Don't forget, let me know if you need help. If I were you, I would kind of just ear hustle today and figure out where you can put your talents to use. Welcome aboard."

Shane went back over to meet with Whitley to finalize some of their ideas.

"Somebody's got a crush," Whitley whispered, looking over at Dustin, who watched Shane walk away.

"No, he's harmless. Plus, I'm seeing somebody," she said before she could catch herself. Her relationship with Coach Rob felt so natural she sometimes forgot that it was a secret.

"You are?" Whitley asked, surprised. "Does he go here?"

Shane realized that she'd said too much. "No, I met him on Friender. He's from Baymont."

"Girl, show me his page. You know they know how to make 'em in BMT."

Shane found herself stuck. She didn't know what to do. She pulled out her phone and connected to Friender. "Dang, the Internet is down. I'll have to show you another time," she lied.

"Okay, Miss Secretive. Show me later, though," Whitley said, giving her a wink.

Old, nosy Whitley. I see why she wants to be a reporter. All up in my business. I can't make that mistake again, Shane thought as the bell rang, signaling transition.

CHAPTER 6

Brandi

Walking down the hall lost in her own thoughts, Brandi didn't even notice that Erick Wright was trying to get her attention. He was one of those people who stood out at PCH. There weren't many white kids at their school, and definitely not one who was as involved as Erick. He wasn't even afraid to go to the hood. He balanced being cool with being smart. He was a true leader. It was rumored that he liked his girls chocolate, but he was never seen with a girl, so nobody could really be sure.

"Brandi, hey," he said as they were passing one another. "Did you see the list they put up for the debate team?"

"Yeah. I saw. I still can't believe it. I thought there was no way I made it. You saw my performance, right?"

"You need to stop. Go check the list again. You're there. Congratulations," Erick said. "I'm the captain this year. We're going to have a great team. You wanna grab a bite and celebrate after school today?"

"No," Brandi said quickly, giving him a nasty look. His face turned sour. "Oh, I'm sorry, Erick ... it's just that ..."

"It's cool," he said, looking disappointed at her obvious diss.

"Shoot," she said, hurrying to her next class. She wasn't trying to be rude to him, but Young Dub had broken her heart. She didn't know what Erick's intentions were, and she wasn't trying to find out. All she wanted was to be on the debate team. She wanted to learn, grow, compete. Make her mark on the world. That was the plan. She didn't have time to be sidetracked, and she was so easily sidetracked that she couldn't take any chances.

There was a meeting after school for those who had won a spot on the team, so she had to see Erick again. Throughout the whole meeting, she was trying to think of something to say to him to smooth over her rude behavior, but she was coming up blank.

After Mr. McAfee finished talking, he asked Erick to come up and say a few words. Brandi could tell that the girls on the team were smitten with him, but they didn't know how to approach him. Dating someone from another race was still something that wasn't too common for black girls. But that boy was so fine!

If you were going to put up with public scrutiny from anybody, he would be the one to make it worth it. He stood six feet tall, had naturally tanned skin, and his eyes changed color with his clothing. He was athletic, smart, and had just enough street smarts in him to go to PCH, but not so much that you had to worry about bringing him home to meet your family.

Brandi looked at him through the other girls' eyes for a moment. She could see why a lot of girls wanted to throw themselves at him, and she was foolish for dismissing his advances. At least she assumed he was making advances at her. *I'm so stupid. The bad ones I keep. The good ones I throw back. Bad timing, Erick, just bad timing.*

He talked a bit about last year's team and the fact that they had almost made it to the state championship in Austin. He planned to get them all the way to state this year, representing Port City.

"Just know that I plan to meet with each of you individually, so don't be surprised if I ask you to do a one-on-one lunch or grab a bite to eat after school. Don't worry. I'll keep your busy schedules in mind. No big deal. I just want to get to know my team," he said, looking directly at Brandi.

She knew if her skin was lighter, he would have been able to see the rosiness of her cheeks. *Thank God for Mama's skin*, she thought. She was truly embarrassed. She had rushed to judgment regarding his intentions, and now she was going to have to eat some humble pie, just like her nana always said.

As soon as Mr. McAfee dismissed them to leave, she went over to talk to Erick. "You got a minute?" she asked.

"Yeah, what is it?" he asked, packing his things away to leave.

"Look, I know I snapped. I was curt." She took a deep breath. "And it's hard to explain why. Just know that it had nothing to do with you, and I'm sorry that it came across that way."

"So it wasn't the cooties sticker on my back?"

"Well, that was part of it." She laughed. She was relieved that they were able to joke about their awkward moment. "So schedule my one-on-one at your leisure and let me know. Cool?"

"Cool." His phone began to ring. "Hey, I gotta take this. Later?"

"Sure." She watched as he walked away. All these years in school together and she never got what so many girls saw in Erick, but today she got it. He was really a cool dude. Too bad she wasn't on the market. But when she was ready, she wanted to find one just like him, preferably with brown skin.

CHAPTER 7

Marisa

Sitting inside the school's dance studio, Marisa felt like a fish out of water. Each of the other girls who had been cast with dance roles in the play was an experienced dancer. She wasn't sure why she had even been chosen. She had no formal dance training. When Mrs. Woods called for the girls to warm up, they knew the whole warm-up routine. Marisa felt like she was playing catch up.

When they began to learn the eight-count for their routine, she found it easier than she had imagined. Once she started relaxing, she was able to concentrate. Her moves became more fluid. Mrs. Woods asked her to perform a duet with another dancer, Sasha. It was like watching synchronized swimming. Even though Sasha had been dancing for years, Marisa held her own. Mrs. Woods and the other girls applauded them when they were finished.

During the break, Sasha approached her. "What studio do you go to?" she asked Marisa.

Marisa looked confused. "I don't go to a studio. I used to take twirling from Miss Honey, but I choreograph my own routines now."

"Wow! You really should be in dance. You're good. I've seen girls who practice for years and don't have the natural ability that you have," Sasha told her.

"Thanks." Marisa was both surprised and happy.

They were able to learn their routine in just one day. It wasn't a huge part of the production, but it needed to be tight.

The drama teacher, Mrs. Scapin, wanted to showcase the best talent in all the creative arts that could be found at PCH. There were even band members who had solos during the show. It was going to be a spectacular play.

When the dancers were done practicing, Mrs. Woods asked Marisa if she could speak with her. "That was quite a performance today. I've watched you twirl for the past three years. I guess I should have known that you could dance too."

"Aw, thanks, Mrs. Woods," Marisa replied. "That's nice of you to say."

"Well, I was thinking about the dance that I originally put together for the role of Tania, and I think it's much too simple now. How about we work together tomorrow and come up with something a little more challenging for you?"

"I'm definitely up for it, Mrs. Woods. Thank you so much."

Marisa was excited about the prospect of dancing onstage. She was thrilled that this world of dance was opening up to her. The arts had always fascinated her. When she arrived the next day to work with Mrs. Woods, the teacher was in the dance studio, working hard. "You ready to see the routine?"

"Sure," Marisa replied.

When Mrs. Woods started dancing as Tania, Marisa was intimidated. She watched as Mrs. Woods moved gracefully and with increased intensity as the character began to pour her heart out to the audience.

When she was done, Marisa was skeptical. "That was awesome, Mrs. Woods, but I don't think I'm going to be able to do that," she said, giggling nervously.

"Anything that you find too difficult, we can modify. Let's get to work."

And work they did. Marisa surprised herself. Even the most challenging portions of the dance were doable. Marisa knew this was going to be a lot of work, but she was sure she could do it.

She was a sweaty mess when she was done. She was also exhausted. She did things she didn't even think were possible, and she enjoyed every minute of it. "Thank you so much, Mrs. Woods. This was so fun."

"I enjoyed it too, Marisa. You are going to do just fine. Anytime you want to practice, you are welcome to come in and work."

"Thanks, Mrs. Woods. Thanks a lot." This play had opened Marisa's eyes to the role that dance could play in her life. She felt as though she was given a second chance. She looked forward to the completion of her reconstructive surgery over the summer, but if it didn't work like the doctor had planned, she knew she would be okay.

I feel like me again. It was as if a weight had been lifted, and she could breathe. In that moment, she thought of Bethany. Marisa knew Bethany would be proud of her for piecing her life back together.

CHAPTER 8

Caught Up

*O*kay, so we have to figure out where we can focus your talent," Shane told Dustin as they sat in Jerry's. There were eating burgers and brainstorming for the yearbook. "The seniors have already stated that they want something fresh and new. We have to deliver."

Dustin had been second in charge of his high school newspaper back in Lake Charles, before moving to Port City. He had walked in Shane's shoes and knew the obstacles that she faced. Even though he had been at the top of the totem pole at his old school, he was willing to take on a smaller role at PCH. He didn't want to step on anyone's toes. All he wanted to do was be a part of the journalism team. After all, journalism was his heart, and he needed it.

"Shane, I'll do anything. Journalism is the only thing that really satisfies me. Without it, I feel lost. So wherever you have the most need, you can put me down in that category."

"Well, you know I have to run it by Whitley, but I think that the freshman team is struggling right now. They need a little guidance, and you may be just the person for the job. You game?"

"I'm down. Whatever you want. You must hear that a lot."

"No," she said shyly. *Okay, now he has to be flirting.*

"You are too modest to be so beautiful."

That does it ... he's flirting. "Look, I should tell you something," Shane started to say, but was interrupted by Robin bringing Aiden to meet her.

Robin was just thankful to have a little quiet time with her fiancé, Gavin. She didn't care why Shane wanted to babysit. After introducing herself to Dustin, Robin quickly headed for the door. "Robie, don't forget his car seat. We are taking them to the park."

Soon after, Dustin's mom arrived with Madison. "You must be Shane. Dustin's told me so much about you." Shane almost choked on her milkshake.

"Not that much, Mom," Dustin said, making a face at her. "I think I can take it from here. You better be going." One thing about being a mixed kid, hiding an embarrassed red-cheeked face was not easy. "She exaggerates," he said to Shane when his mother left.

After the kids got sugared up on ice cream, they went over to the park to let them run it off.

"Your mom is whiter than mine," Shane commented as they sat on a park bench, watching the little ones play.

"Yeah, most people look at mixed kids like they are all black or all white. They can't understand the melting pot on the inside unless they live it."

"Yeah, I know what you mean. People used to think I was so different. There was a time when I had trouble making friends, but once I found Brandi and Marisa, it just felt right. I remember once when I stayed the night with one of my mom's friends, I overheard her grumbling about not knowing what to do with my hair. It hurt my feelings back then because it reminded me that I was different. Today, I would probably laugh."

"I've had my share of those moments too, but I wouldn't change a thing. I love my diversity. I've found a way to use it to my advantage."

They rounded up the children and

headed for home. Dustin dropped Shane and Aiden back at the house just in time for Aiden's dinner, bath, and bedtime.

"So, maybe we can try this again without the little ones," he suggested.

"Um, I'm kind of seeing somebody right now, Dustin. I don't want to give you the wrong impression." She tiptoed through the conversation. She liked Dustin, but not like that. She kept wishing he would stop trying to push her.

"Oh, I didn't know. Hey, I'm sorry. This just felt so ... easy."

Yeah, too easy. He didn't know Shane liked things more complicated. There was no danger in dating Dustin. She needed danger. She lived for it.

The next day at school she tried to avoid him as much as possible. If it hadn't been for the debacle with the freshman group's layout, she may not have had to see him at all. They both worked feverishly to fix what the freshman team had presented to the group.

"It's like there's no talent in their group," Shane complained to Dustin and Whitley.

"Just give them some time," Dustin told her. "It's their first year in a program like this. I'm sure they'll surprise you next year."

"Well, I need a break," Shane told them. "I'm going to the vending machine. Do y'all want anything?"

After they declined her offer, she headed out to see Coach Rob. *I need more than a soda if I'm going to get through this.*

Coach Rob was in his office with Kylie, going over some of the scholarship offers that she had received. Kylie was all smiles until she saw Shane walk in. "What?" she snapped.

"Really, Kylie? Get a life." The two of them seemed to be at odds ever since Shane joined the volleyball team.

"You two need to try to get along. You

are setting a bad example for the other girls on the volleyball team. Especially you, Kylie. You're the captain."

"It's not volleyball season, Coach," Shane said smartly.

"Kylie, will you give me a minute to talk to Shane, please?"

"No." He looked at her sternly and she gave in. "All right, all right. I'll just be in the gym," she said before leaving.

"I can't stand her. What is she doing in here anyway?" Shane asked him suspiciously.

"What did it look like she was doing? We were going over scholarship opportunities for her. It's something that we have to do for you next year too."

"So what else are you doing for her?" Shane's pulse was beginning to quicken. She could feel herself becoming angry.

"Hey, don't be so insecure," he told her. "You know you're the only girl for me." He went over to where she was sitting and kneeled down next to the chair. He gently pecked her lips and looked at her in a way that knocked her defensive wall down.

She was shocked and surprised when the door opened and Dustin was standing in the doorway.

"Oh, I'm sorry," he stammered uncomfortably. "Kylie told me you were in here. I was just ... um ... about to leave."

Shane couldn't tell how much he had witnessed, but she knew he had seen something. Coach Rob stood up immediately, towering over Dustin, who was not a small guy either. But compared to Coach Rob, a grown man, he looked like a little kid. "We were just finishing up. Shane, let me know if you need anything else."

"Yes, sir," she said, trying to sound studious.

"Are you okay?" Dustin asked as they left Coach's office. "It looked like he was trying to kiss you. I've met men like him before and—"

"Just drop it, Dustin. It's okay." She tried to reassure him without saying too much.

"It's okay? Shane, please don't tell me that this is the guy you were talking about. Shane—"

"It's none of your business, Dustin. I said drop it. Please." She walked away from him abruptly, hurried to the journalism room, gathered her things, and left campus. She couldn't believe that they had been so sloppy. Kylie knew exactly what she was doing sending Dustin in there. *I really hope he doesn't open his big mouth.*

CHAPTER 9

Shane

Shane walked down the stairs to join her family for breakfast before heading off to school. She looked terrible. She had not slept all night. Thoughts of Dustin telling someone about his suspicions of her and Coach Rob were swimming through her head. She tried to make herself feel better. How much could he have actually seen?

Her father was the first to notice how tired she looked. "You feeling okay, Shane?" he asked as she slumped down in her chair, grabbing a bagel to nibble.

"Yeah, I just had trouble sleeping last night. I have an article to finish for the school newspaper, and it's stressing me out. Deadline is this afternoon."

"Is there anything Dad can do to help you out? You know that I ran the newspaper when I was in high school."

"I know, Dad. You've told me a hundred times," she said, rolling her eyes.

"Brian, leave the girl alone," her mother stepped in, kissing her daughter on the forehead. "Nobody wants to hear about your glory days this morning."

"I'm just trying to help, but I see you ladies have this under control. Shane, I'm here if you need any help, though." He winked at her.

"Go to work, Daddy. Port City needs you more than I do right now. I can take care of my own problems."

"Now that's the Shane I know. Take care of your business, my baby."

She felt guilty telling her dad a lie, but

she couldn't exactly tell him the truth. She had already completed her article and reviewed the others from her team. There was nothing on her mind but Dustin and Coach Rob.

Usually when she had problems, her dad was her sounding board, but not today. Today she had to put her big girl panties on and face the heat.

When she arrived at school, Dustin was waiting by her locker. His face looked solemn. She knew he was going to want to talk to her. She just didn't realize that it would be first thing in the morning.

"Hey," she said nonchalantly, as if there wasn't a huge elephant in a tutu standing in the middle of the hall.

"Hey, Shane, you think we could go somewhere and talk?" he asked.

"I have class, Dustin. I can't."

"Oh, now you want to follow the rules?" he asked sarcastically.

"What do you want from me?" She threw her books in her locker. His concern was starting to anger her.

"I want you to tell me the truth. Is Coach Rob trying to talk you into doing something that you aren't comfortable with?"

"What's wrong with you?" she whispered. "Don't say that!" She pulled him into an empty classroom. "You are going to get me into trouble," she said to him once they were alone.

"You won't be in trouble, Shane. *He* will. It looked like he was pushing up on you. He's too old for that. You have to turn him in."

"I will not," she spat. "I'll take care of this, Dustin. I'm a big girl."

"Okay," he said, breathing a sigh of relief. "But if you need me, I have your back." He looked at Shane with eyes she had seen before. *Oh no, he's falling for me.*

Can't I just have one guy friend who doesn't fall in love with me?

When Dustin left to go to class, Shane sent a text to Brandi and Marisa. "911. Room B123." Within minutes, both of them appeared in the doorway.

"What's wrong?" Brandi asked anxiously, wearing a set of plastic gloves as if she had come to do surgery.

"Dang, girl, I didn't call for a doctor."

"Shut it. I was just about to start my lab. I just told Mrs. Smith that I had an emergency and ran out of the class. What happened? Why the nine-one-one?"

Marisa closed her eyes, examining the situation. She couldn't understand what could be so urgent. They were still in first period. "Talk, Shane. What's going on?"

Shane didn't know where to begin. Her friends had been adamant about her staying away from Coach Rob. She had made them believe that she had done just that. But right now, she needed advice. She couldn't tell anybody besides her two best friends what she was going through, and it sure did beat going to therapy.

"I'm still seeing Coach Rob," she blurted out as if she had wanted to tell them for weeks.

"Well, duh," Brandi said, removing her lab gloves. "I told you, Mari."

"Shane, I thought Brandi was crazy when she said you were still seeing him. I never dreamed—"

"Oh, get over it, Mari. You know Shane plays by her own rules. It's going to take more than li'l ole us telling her to leave him alone. Now spill it. What happened?"

"I think we got caught."

"Oh no." It was more than Marisa could take. She sat down on one of the stools in the classroom.

Shane told them her story. She told them about their private encounters in his office, about sneaking out of Brandi's house, about Dustin walking in on the two of them yesterday, and his threat to expose Coach Rob.

"I don't want any part of this," Marisa told them. "I can't imagine that creep putting his hands on you. What Coach is doing is plain wrong. And he knows it. He's a predator, Shane. It's disgusting."

"Go to class, Mari," Brandi told her. "Let me and Shane talk for a bit."

"Gladly," Marisa told them. "Shane, just be careful."

Marisa was determined not to wind up a statistic, and if she had to drag Shane and Brandi with her kicking and screaming, she planned to do so. For this man to come into their lives and try to ruin one of her friends, it was unthinkable.

Shane and Brandi sat and talked everything out. Brandi wasn't as much of a wild child as Shane, but she definitely walked the line more than Marisa, who embraced the good girl role with open arms.

"Okay, you have to leave dude alone. I don't know what spell he has over you, but he's not even all that."

"You crazy. He's like a mix between Shemar Moore, Drake, and—"

"Pee-wee Herman. He could never have pulled a girl like you when he was in school, so he's trying to use his authority to get you now. You have to face it, Shane. He's using you."

Shane let Brandi's words sink in. *Maybe she's right. Is he just using me?*

She thought about everything that Brandi said. She couldn't keep her mind on school for the rest of the day. She was so happy when the day finished. She had a yearbook meeting after school, but she knew she should talk to Coach Rob before she went.

When she arrived at his office, Kylie was in there. Again. She was laughing way too hard and twirling her hair. Shane could tell that she was flirting with Coach

Rob, but she couldn't tell if he was getting the hint or not.

"Hey, can I speak with you a second, Coach?"

"Sure. Kylie, will you give us a minute?"

Kylie stomped out of his office, and he immediately turned to Shane. "Did you talk to your little friend? Dusty, is it?"

"Yeah. He thinks that you are trying to push up on me."

"I am," he said, grabbing her seductively.

"Stop, Rob. Seriously, I don't want you to get into any trouble. We have to stop this."

He moved away from her like a little boy who had been put on a time-out. "Is that what you want? I thought you could handle this. You're going to let him keep us apart. Really, Shane? I thought you were coming here to tell me that you had this handled."

"I do have it handled. I think."

"Well, *know* that it's handled. Don't

come back here until you know." He slapped her on the butt. "Now let me get back to work." He opened the door to let her out. "Kylie, you can come back now."

Shane walked across the gym, watching the way Coach Rob interacted with Kylie. She had a horrible feeling about the two of them, and she was determined that this fool wasn't about to play her, teacher or not.

She was late for her journalism meeting, but she took the chair closest to Whitley so that she could jump right in. She wanted to think about something other than Coach Rob. When they broke off into groups, Dustin made a beeline for her. "You okay? Why were you late?"

"Dustin, you are the biggest snoop. I'm okay. I took care of that little situation. I won't have a problem with Coach Rob ever again."

"Good. I don't wanna have to knock out Old School."

She winced when she heard the nick-name he gave Coach Rob, but she couldn't let him see that. She knew she had to spend less time with Dustin. He was a smart kid, and she didn't need him all up in her business.

When she left to go to the restroom, she forgot her phone. She was okay with that. She kept it locked, so nobody could be in her stuff. She hadn't banked on Coach Rob sending her a text, and she really hadn't banked on Dustin reading it. It read, "I ♥ u. Don't eva let sumbody com b/t us again."

Dustin grabbed his jacket and was gone before Shane even returned.

"Where's Dustin?" she asked Whitley.

Whitley never took her eyes off the article she was reading. "I don't know ... he mumbled something about an old school and left. He said he had to take care of something."

Shane grabbed her phone. It was still

locked. She opened it and read the text from Coach Rob. Surely Dustin hadn't seen it. How could he? Her phone was locked.

As she looked at her phone, a message popped up from Dustin, "U played me." She didn't have to unlock it to read it. Oh no! Dustin could have read Coach Rob's message the same way. This situation was getting out of control.

CHAPTER 10

Brandi

When Brandi arrived at debate practice, she noticed Dustin leaning against the wall next to the auditorium. She knew he had to be there because of Shane. Their girl code didn't allow her to speak to him before speaking to Shane, so she had to get rid of him quickly.

"Hey, Dustin," she said, attempting to ease past him as if she didn't know he was there to talk to her.

"Brandi, can I talk to you for a second?"

She looked at her phone as though she

didn't know the time. "I have two minutes. I can't be late for practice."

"It'll only take a second." She could tell that he was searching for words. "Has Shane told you anything about Coach Rob?"

"Coach Rob?" she asked, pretending to be confused. "Who's that again? Oh yeah, Shane's volleyball coach. I remember him."

"I don't know how to say this, but I think that he's ... um ... trying to holler at Shane. Like romantically." He brought his voice down to a whisper.

"You don't have to worry about Shane. She's a big girl."

"Yeah, but he's a grown man."

"Look, Dustin, I'll talk to Shane. I'm sure it's nothing."

"It is something!" he yelled. "That's what I'm trying to get you to see."

"Don't you dare come here yelling at me. Now chill out!" Brandi was truly her mama's child, and she knew how to defend herself.

Erick Wright heard the commotion and came out of the auditorium just as Brandi was yelling at Dustin.

"Is everything okay?" Erick asked, looking at Brandi and sizing Dustin up at the same time. Brandi was relieved that he had come out of the auditorium when he had. She wanted to be as far away from Dustin as possible. Shane had raved about how cool he was, and how much they had in common. Brandi was getting a different picture. Something was off here, and she couldn't put her finger on it. "Brandi, are you okay?" Erick asked again, standing in between her and Dustin.

She nodded her head, but she looked a bit shaken up. *Dustin is a creep. I've met creeps before.* She started thinking about Steven, the guy who had kidnapped her during her freshman year. She started to project her feelings about Steven onto

Dustin. The more she saw the same characteristics in Dustin, the more she wanted to scratch his eyeballs out. She pushed Erick out of her way. "Dustin, I'm going to say this to you, and I need you to believe me. If Shane ever tells me that you so much as look at her wrong, you will regret it for the rest of your life. Do you understand me?"

"I'm not the bad guy, Brandi. I'm trying to help Shane."

"You barely know her!" Brandi screeched. Erick grabbed her arm as she moved closer to Dustin.

"Hey, Brandi, come in the auditorium. It's over," Erick said to her calmly, trying to get her to back down.

"You're going to regret this, Brandi," Dustin warned her.

"Was that supposed to be a threat? Are you threatening me?" She started to become hysterical.

"Hey, guy, you gotta move around," Erick told him.

"Dude, that's not how I meant it," Dustin said, trying to reason with Erick.

"Well then, be careful with your words," Erick said, looking at him man-to-man.

Even though Brandi had put on her bravest face while Dustin was there, when he left, she began to cry uncontrollably. Erick held her in his arms as she just let it go. One of the students from the debate team came out of the auditorium to check on him, but Erick just shook his head. When Brandi was done crying, he sat next to her on the ground.

"Why are you so upset? What happened between you and this guy?"

"I can't really talk about it."

"You really can tell me, Brandi."

No, I really can't. "The short version ... he's Shane's friend, but I think he would like to be more than that. It just doesn't seem like a healthy crush. He's creepy."

"What did he do to make you think he's a creep?"

She thought about it and couldn't articulate it to him. "It's just a feeling I have. I don't know, and I don't know him. He transferred to Port City this year. I want to know why he left Louisiana. I need to know more about him than he knows about us. Ya know?"

"Mind if I help you figure it out?"

She was happy to have an ally, and even happier that it was Erick. "Sure," she told him. "I think that's a good idea." She smiled at him, and he led her into the auditorium so they could get to work.

CHAPTER 11

Marisa

*M*arisa was always a person who was slow to anger. The problem occurred *after* she got angry, and Dustin Chaisson had pissed her off. After what Brandi told her, she was dead set on finding him. Nobody, absolutely nobody, was going to scare Brandi like Steven did. Brandi had been through enough.

"There's something wrong with the guy that Shane's hanging out with. I can just feel it, Mari."

"What makes you think that, Bran?"

"Number one, he was at the auditorium

waiting for me to get to debate practice. I don't even know how he knew that I was in debate."

"He could have found that out anywhere. Shane could have told him."

"Let me finish. Then he started asking all these questions about Shane and Coach Rob. I didn't give him the answers he was looking for, and he just turned on me. His face became angry, and he started yelling at me.

"You know me. Once that happened, the claws came out. I started getting in his face, but I have to tell you, he was really scaring me. I was so happy when Erick came out of the auditorium. It just didn't feel like a regular argument. He was borderline stalkerish. Obsessive even."

"Do you think he would hurt Shane?"

"I really don't know. People do crazy things all the time." Brandi got that faraway gaze in her eyes, and Marisa knew she was really talking about Steven. Brandi had never completely dealt with her feelings about being kidnapped.

Later, Marisa mulled over her conversation with Brandi. She had to see this Dustin for herself. She had to see what he was capable of. There was no way that she was going to stand by and allow him to hurt Brandi or Shane. When she saw him coming down the hallway, she started walking toward him.

"Hey, Dustin? Can I have a word with you?"

"Sure, Marisa." He let out a huge sigh. "Is this about Shane?"

"Yes, but Brandi too."

"Oh yeah, that. Hey, I'm sorry about how that went down. I was just all worked up about Shane."

"A little too worked up, wouldn't you say?" Marisa replied.

"Maybe," he said, studying his feet.

"You really need to back off my girls,"

Marisa continued. "I'm the last person in the world who looks for a confrontation, but you are spooking both of them out. I'm not about to stand by and watch them get hurt."

Her words seemed to shock Dustin. "Me? Hurt them? I would never. I'm the one looking out for Shane. I don't know what she's told you, but it's that creepy coach who's trying to hurt her."

Marisa had her own reservations about Coach Rob, but she wasn't about to share them with Dustin, even though she could see where he was coming from.

"Hey, look. Shane is a big girl, and Brandi and I both have her back. You need to give her a little space. I don't think that she's looking for a hero, ya know?"

"Yeah, I kinda got that. I'll tell you what," Dustin offered. "I'll back off, but you have to promise me that if she needs my help, you'll let me know."

Marisa agreed with Dustin. She was

sure she would never need to ask for his help, but it was a nice gesture. She was just as concerned about Shane as Dustin was. She couldn't understand why Brandi thought that he was so dangerous. She wasn't getting "creepy, stalker guy" from him. She started to worry about Brandi. At some point, Brandi was going to have to deal with her own issues.

Marisa felt confused after her conversation with Brandi, but now she was even more confused after talking to Dustin. Right smack dab in the middle of all this confusion was Shane, who seemed to not care about anything but pleasing Coach Rob. Surely her friend wasn't really falling for that user. If so, this was only the tip of the iceberg. *Can't we have one semester of peace?* Marisa thought as she placed her books back into her locker.

CHAPTER 12

The Note

It was the week before spring break, and there was a joyful buzz in the air. Everyone eagerly awaited the much-needed vacation after preparing tirelessly for the state examinations. Those were scheduled to take place a few days after they returned from the break. The state was always changing the tests, making them more complicated and difficult for students to pass. It was as if they wanted them to fail. But what would they gain from that?

As Shane, Marisa, and Brandi filed into the auditorium, they had one thought on their minds, ditch their class and teachers and find each other. There was no way they were going to go through an entire assembly without linking up. Today's program was obviously about the state exam.

"I really don't feel like sitting through another lecture about passing a test," Shane complained. "These discussions are always so lame."

"You think everything about high school is lame this year except for Coach Rob-ing the cradle," Brandi snapped at her.

"You not funny, trick."

"No, she kinda is," Marisa said, laughing with Brandi.

"I should have stayed with my class," Shane said, rolling her eyes. "Look, my boo thang," she said when Coach Rob entered the auditorium with his class. "Ew, is that Kylie again? Seriously, she gotta back-back."

"Girl, you ain't giving it up. You know you not his only, right?" Brandi asked, trying to bring her friend back to reality.

"She's right, Shane," Marisa chimed in.

The principal came to the stage to announce their guest speaker. As soon as she stepped foot on the stage, they could hear one of Beaty's signature beats coming through the speakers. "Aw, dats my boy," Shane hollered over the loud music. Beaty and Young Dub were the dynamic duo of Port City rap. Beaty was the producer and Dub was the rapper.

"Seriously?" Brandi mouthed, rolling her eyes. There was a time when she would have been excited too, but the thought of Young Dub walking out on that stage still made her heart drop a little.

Just last semester she had been dating Young Dub, but he had broken her heart by cheating on her with the female rapper Lil Flo, who most guys in Port City would have given their right arm to date. Brandi knew that if Beaty was around, there was a chance that Dub would be too.

Luckily for Brandi, it was not Young

Dub. Another rapper appeared on the stage and did cover music. He took one of Young Dub's newest club bangers and turned it into a song about passing their state examination. Surprisingly, the whole student body was getting into the program. By the time his show was over, the students knew the words to his songs and were rapping about passing their test.

"That was cool," Marisa said to her friends as they lined up to exit the auditorium.

"I liked it too. It beat going to gym."

"B, you have to be the only person who doesn't like P.E. You're a cheerleader! Who doesn't like P.E.?" Shane asked her.

"Me," Brandi told her abruptly. "I am not down with nappy edges. I'm not trying to sweat in the middle of the day. They doin' too much."

They finally started to move when a student came down the row of seats next to them. "Are you Shane?" she asked.

"Yeah, who wants to know?"

"This guy asked me to give you this." She handed her a note with "Shane Foster" written on it.

"Is that from your stalker?" Brandi teased her.

"Dustin may be weird, but he's *not* a stalker," Shane said as she opened the note. "Tell her, Mari." Marisa just shrugged her shoulders.

"Shane?" Mari asked as she noticed her friend's reaction to the letter. She jerked it from her hands and shared it with Brandi. The note simply read:

May 1 is D-day:
Brandi, Shane, Marisa, Coach Rob, Mrs. Monroe
You will be dealt with. This is not a threat.
It's a promise. Don't sleep.

"What does this mean? Don't sleep?" Marisa asked, confused.

"I don't know, but I'm certain Dustin

has something to do with it," Brandi told her friends. "So, do you believe me now, Shane? Or you still on Team Dustin?"

"Dustin wouldn't send this," she told Brandi. But who would? They slowly looked around the auditorium. Everyone looked different now. They all looked guilty, suspect, dangerous even.

"We have to tell someone," Marisa told them, but the fire alarm startled them back to reality. "Oh no, this is too crazy."

"That's not a drill," Shane told her friends. "Let's get out of here. I have a bad feeling about this."

They left school in Brandi's old, beat-up car that her mother had bought her when she got her driver's license. It didn't have air-conditioning or a radio, but it sure did come in handy when they needed a ride.

They rode in silence for much of the trip and decided to go to the seawall, where they could think clearly. The air coming off the water always had a calming effect. They avoided the part of the seawall where Marisa had her accident earlier in the school year. It was still sad for them.

"Why would anybody want to hurt any of us?" Marisa asked, throwing a rock into the water.

"It's probably just a prank," Shane said.

"Let me see it again," Brandi said. "For some reason, I don't think this is a prank, Shane."

"This is serious. We have to get back to the campus and tell somebody," Marisa warned them. "It's not just our names on the list. There are teachers too. Look, Coach Rob—"

"Who would want to hurt Coach Rob? This is his first year here, and Mrs. Monroe? Seriously," Shane said, trying to think it through.

"Dustin," Brandi said, having a moment of clarity. "The kid is twisted. Y'all didn't see his ugly side. I did."

Marisa was reluctant to agree with

Brandi. When she met with Dustin, she didn't get that vibe. "Brandi, you are too quick to blame him. I'm sorry. I just don't see it. He seemed ... I don't know ... genuine."

"I don't know anymore. This is just too much," Shane told them.

"Well, I know. Dustin is creepy and stalkerish, and we didn't have this problem before he came here."

"Okay, but what if you are wrong, B?" Marisa asked. "This is not one of those situations that we can handle by ourselves. We have to tell somebody."

"Girl, they are gonna wanna know why we think it's Dustin. You tryin' to get my name and Coach Rob's all up on the front page of the *Port City Tribune* or worse yet, the *Messenger*? You know how they love to rub the Foster name in the dirt."

Shane was torn. Turn the letter in and face the music about her relationship with Coach Rob. Don't turn the letter in and take their chances with a potential psycho. "Look, let's get out of here. May first is forever away. Surely he will show his hand before then. When he does, he'll be the one getting dealt with."

"I hope you're right, Shane. I just hope you are right." Marisa shook her head. She had a bad feeling, just like she had when Brandi was "dating" the guy on the Internet. She wasn't about to let it happen again, even if it meant outing Shane. Her friends wouldn't listen to her, and she didn't want to betray them, but she didn't want anything to happen to either one of them. She couldn't lose another friend.

"She is right. Just don't do anything stupid, Mari," Brandi warned her. "Let us handle this. I'm wearing my detective hat, and I'm going to get to the bottom of this. I will not be duped by some lunatic."

"Again," Marisa reminded her.

"Hey, y'all chill out. The last thing we need to do is let this divide us," Shane told them as they headed back to the school. Again, they rode in silence. Trusting anybody was going to be difficult at this point, but they had to act normal. When they got to the student parking lot, Shane stopped them before they went back into the school. "Hey, it's not lost on me that this is my fault. I'm just sorry that my … um … extracurricular activities are affecting the two of you. I'd die if anything happened to you."

"Hopefully, you won't have to prove it," Marisa said, shaking her head.

"We're going to be okay," Brandi told them both. "We always are, right?"

They thought about all they had been through and what they had survived. They knew Brandi was right. She just had to be.

CHAPTER 13

Shane

As Shane prepared for her date with Dustin, her hands trembled as she applied mascara to her eyelashes. She shook her hands, as if that would somehow allow her to regain control of her own limbs. The girls had devised the plan for Shane to go out with Dustin during spring break to pick his brain for information. Shane had assured her friends that she would be careful and safe.

Now, as the time approached for her to be alone with him, she was getting more afraid that she could be wrong. *What if he does want to harm me? What if I wind up like Brandi did, held prisoner in this guy's basement or something? There are no basements in Port City, dummy.* Her thoughts were running away from her. She wanted to tell Robin what was going on, but she was afraid that her sister would ask too many questions or try to talk her out of it.

When the doorbell rang, she felt her heart drop into her stomach. "Come on, Shane, get it together," she told herself aloud as she stared into the mirror. When she ran down the stairs to meet Dustin, there was no sign remaining of the nervous jitters that she felt while getting ready.

She looked at him in his button-down Ralph Lauren shirt and his sagging khakis, looking clean-cut and wholesome. Her fears quickly began to subside. *I can't be scared of this dude. He's a journalism geek like me. Harmless.* She tried to convince herself, but the weakness she felt in her knees told the real story. In his eyes, she saw her new friend. The boy she had connected with on so many levels, not the picture of the monster that Brandi had painted.

"Okay, let's blow this Popsicle stand," she told him, grabbing a sweater from the coat rack.

"Come back at a decent hour tonight, Shane," her mother told her before kissing her daughter.

"I'll do my best," Shane said, knowing that curfew was a non-issue.

"You were right, my mom is way whiter than yours," Dustin laughed. Kimberly Foster was hip, cool, and as urban as you could get and still be white.

"She a'ight. I like her," Shane replied with a grin.

"Okay, so you wanted to go out. What's the plan?" he asked her.

Shane's wheels were turning. The real plan was to show him the letter and gauge his reaction. The girls figured that if he was cornered, they could get him to confess. Shane convinced her friends that she knew how to work this boy over, even if she had to pull out every trick Mrs. Scapin had taught her during drama class.

"I'm hungry. But I know Jerry's is too packed during spring break. You know any cool spots?" Shane asked.

"There's a new restaurant in the mall. Is that too packed for you too?"

The mall was perfect. She needed a location that wasn't too noisy, but at the same time wasn't too empty, just in case he lost it.

Once they arrived, they ordered a few appetizers to munch on while they talked. They looked like two young people having a wonderful time. But soon after their food arrived, Shane pushed her plate away.

"What's wrong? You don't like it? We can order something different."

"No, it's not that. I just lost my appetite." Shane stared at a fork on the table.

"Why? You're making me nervous, Shane. What's wrong?"

"I'm scared to tell you. I don't want to involve anybody who doesn't need to be involved." She brought her voice down to a whisper. "I'm scared." She looked nervously around the restaurant, as if someone was spying on them.

Now Dustin joined her in putting his fork down. He moved to her side of the table so that he could hear her better. The closeness of his body made her even more nervous. *I could be breaking bread with a crazy person,* she thought.

"Talk to me. Is it Coach Rob?"

"No, it's not Coach Rob." She almost came out of character, but quickly realized that she could not show her true colors. She slowly pulled the note out of her pocket and placed it on the table. She kept her hand on it as she said, "What I'm about to show you has to stay between the two of us, okay?"

He agreed and she passed him the note. He read it slowly and then a second time. "Who knows about this?"

She found his question odd. "Nobody."

"Not even your friends?"

"No, I didn't want to endanger them too."

"Their names are on this list, Shane. It's a little too late for that. When did you get this? Who gave it to you?"

"Honestly, I don't know the girl. I think she was a ninth grader. She looked really young, and I'd never seen her before. She approached me in the auditorium during that program."

"You've had this for almost a week, and you didn't show the principal? We need to go to the police. Come on. I'm getting the check."

Shane didn't want to leave the comfort of the crowded restaurant and mall. She still wasn't sure if Dustin was behind the note. She forced herself to cry. He seemed to sense that she was in real pain. "Don't cry. Everything is going to be okay. I won't let anything happen to you. You can believe that."

She didn't know what to believe. *Is he trying to get me alone? Does he want the police to question Coach Rob? Omigod, that's it. There's no real threat at all. He's doing this to get back at Rob.*

"I'm not going to the police."

"Why?" Just then, a lightbulb went off for Dustin. "You are trying to protect him, aren't you? You have a hit out on you, and you are protecting him. Did you tell him about the list?"

"Nobody knows, Dustin. I swear," she lied, crossing her fingers under the table.

"Shane, listen. This could be really serious. You can't hide this, especially not for him. This man is playing you. Don't be naïve. You are better than this."

"I am not." *Wait, that didn't come out right.* "He's not playing me."

"Are you silly enough to think that you're the first student he's pursued? Are you?" He threw twenty-five dollars on the table to pay for their food. "Hey, I'm not going to stand by and watch him make a fool of you." The temper that he had revealed to Brandi started to come out again. Shane could tell he was losing control. It was the perfect time to pounce.

"No, you are the one trying to make a fool of me."

"Come again? How exactly am I doing that?"

"I know you are behind this note, Dustin." Her eyes narrowed as she stared at him. "Nobody else knows about me and Rob. You'd do anything to break us up."

"So, it's you and Rob now? Shane, get over yourself! I was trying to help you. I was going to spare your feelings, but whatever. This is the man that you are so in love with." He took a sheet of paper out of his pocket. When Shane opened the paper, there was an old newspaper article with Coach Rob's picture. The headline read, "Teacher Being Investigated for Inappropriate Relationship with Student."

"You are such a liar, Dustin! That's Photoshopped."

"Believe that if you want to. You know what, Shane? Good luck with your stalker, your man-friend, and your silly little girlfriends who probably put you up to this whole charade. You're all stupid. Just leave me out of this." He walked away from the table, disgusted.

"Can I still get a ride home?" she yelled. But he threw his hands up in the air and walked out.

Shane slumped down in the booth and stared at the article Dustin had given her. She studied the photo and the picture that the article painted of Coach Rob. It was as if his eyes were staring back at her. *This can't be real. You couldn't have done all these horrible things.*

CHAPTER 14

Brandi

$\mathcal{B}$randi pulled up to the mall and saw Shane sitting on the bench waiting for her while playing on her phone. She knew her friend so well.

"Step away from *Words with Friends* and get in the car!" Shane rolled her eyes, not at Brandi, but at the situation. "Didn't go so well, eh?"

"No, not at all. Now I know what you felt like when Brendon kicked your butt to the curb," Shane said, joking about a disastrous date Brandi had endured.

"Oh, you bringing up the past now. Don't go there, Shane Renée."

"Nah, on the real, though. I don't feel like I know any more than before. Either Dustin is a really good liar, or he didn't do it. Look at what he gave me."

"I'm driving, woman. Read it to me."

Robert Reynolds was dismissed today by Briar Creek Independent School District for inappropriate relations with a student.

His relationship was revealed by the student's aunt, who he was also dating at the time.

The student claimed that she was approached by Reynolds when he pulled her out of class. At that time, he started getting her out of class more and more often, making her do things she was not comfortable doing. She stated that she was afraid of him and didn't want to hurt her aunt.

The student claimed he threatened

her on numerous occasions, saying that he would tell everyone that she had been the one coming on to him. The student felt that she had to continue the relationship, or he would ruin her life.

Reynolds was not available for a comment at this time.

"There's even a picture of him," Shane said.

Brandi drove in disbelief as Shane read the article. "So you're not the first student that he's been courting? Wow, that girl could be you, Shane."

"That would never be me, Brandi. I'm not that dumb."

They pulled up to Shane's house, but Brandi decided not to get out. "Hey, it's late. I need to get back to Raven. She needs quality time with her sissy. You know how that goes."

"Well, thank you for rescuing me."

"Anytime. I know you'd do it for me."

"Correction, I have done it for you," Shane said, remembering how she and Robin had found Brandi shivering on the curb during ninth grade after Brendon kicked her out of his car. At least Dustin had left her at the mall. It wasn't December, so she wasn't frozen to the core.

Brandi drove home, wondering if she was wrong about Dustin. But she quickly dismissed the thought. She was sure the guy was a certifiable psycho after the tirade she witnessed that day at the auditorium. She just had to prove it.

She wanted to figure out his motives. He wasn't the only one who knew how to work the Internet. She could too.

When she got home, she Googled his name. What she read, she didn't like. When she finally got a photograph to go along with his story, she knew she had found the right person. "Hello, Dustin Chaisson," she said as she stared at his mug shot. She copied the link and added it to the folder she had created on her computer. She knew her friends would believe her now.

He was the monster she thought he was, and now she could prove it.

She picked up her phone and asked Erick to come over to her house. He was there within the hour. Since she found Dustin's mug shot, she was also able to uncover the story that went along with it. Erick was impressed with her investigative skills.

"This is some good information that you've found, Brandi. I wonder why his records aren't sealed. He's still a minor. That's kinda messed up."

"No, he was tried as an adult. He even pleaded guilty, so you know he did it."

"He attacked this lady in her home? That's crazy. This dude is seriously demented. I'm really happy that I intervened when he had you cornered in the hallway. There's no telling what he would have done."

"The boy went from two to ten on me in a matter of seconds. I'm telling you, there's a wire loose or something. I didn't even tell you that he left Shane at the mall the other night."

"Why was Shane with him?"

"The short version? She was trying to get him to confess to writing the list."

"What list?"

"Shoot." As always, Brandi had said too much. They had been talking about the list so much that she forgot she wasn't supposed to say anything.

"Spill it, Brandi. What list?"

"Okay, okay ... but you can't tell anybody. Before we left for spring break, some girl passed Shane a note. It had a list of people on it who were 'going to be dealt with.'"

"What? Did you turn it in to Mrs. Montgomery?"

"No." Brandi knew she couldn't go into detail about why they chose to keep it a secret. "Look, it's complicated, okay? We had to try and figure it out on our own."

"You girls are playing with fire."

"Yeah, well, we've had our share of burns before. You'd be surprised at how fast you can heal when you have to."

CHAPTER 15

Marisa

Happy to see Port City from the plane, Marisa was glad to be returning home. She took out her tablet and opened her Friender page. "I ♥ goin to L.A. But seeing Port City is like no other feelin'. Welcome home to me." She put her tablet away and started to put her things back in her carry-on bag. "Mama, we are about to land."

"Um-hm," her mother said groggily, trying to will her eyes to open. It had been another long trip, and Marisa could tell that it was wearing on her mother.

She watched her mother as she rested.

She knew that her mom was sacrificing for her by flying back and forth to California. Her mother was a homebody. After all, she had only been a U.S. citizen for a little over a year now. Traveling had not been an option for her when she was not legal. They took a few family trips within Texas, but that was about it. Now she was jet-setting back and forth across half the country.

Marisa sometimes felt bad that her mother's attention had to be focused on her and not on her brother or sisters, but it was necessary. She had to get rid of these scars. The job with the Beverly Hills plastic surgeon Marisa's agent had gotten for her had opened the door to do just that.

The flight attendant instructed the passengers to stow their items and put their chairs upright. A few minutes later the plane landed with a jolt, waking her mother completely. "Okay, now we are home," Mrs. Maldonado said.

Her mother let out a long sigh and began to collect her own things. Once they got to baggage claim, they grabbed their suitcases. Then they returned to their parked car.

When they finally pulled up at home, they were both equally relieved and exhausted. Marisa was just happy that there were a couple of days left of spring break. Going to school right after having another round of treatment on her face seemed impossible.

When they pulled into the driveway, Marisa noticed someone on the porch. She couldn't make out who it was, but it was obviously a guy. As they got closer, she realized that it was Dustin, Shane's friend. *How does this guy know where I live?* She was automatically put off by his presence.

"Hey, Dustin, what's up?" she asked nonchalantly, like his loitering at her house was totally normal.

He looked a mess, and he was talking

rapidly. "You have to talk to Shane, Marisa. She will listen to you."

"Dustin, slow down. What are you talking about?"

"She didn't show you the article I gave her about Coach Rob?"

"I'm just getting back from California. I've been kinda busy," she said, pointing to the bandages on her face. "Can you just tell me about it yourself, please?"

He handed her a copy of the article. He searched her face as she read. "Do you see? This guy is a predator, and Shane's falling for him. She won't listen to me, but maybe you'll have some luck."

"You don't know Shane well at all, do you?" Marisa laughed, even though she knew that the situation wasn't funny. "I'll see what she has to say about it, Dustin, but I can't make Shane do anything. Nobody can."

"God!" he screamed, tilting his head to

the sky. His sudden frustration alarmed Marisa. "The three of you are nuts! Shane, especially Brandi, and now you too. I thought that out of any of them, you would have my back on this."

Dustin grew increasingly agitated. "You three girls. You are all too smart for your own good. I can't even believe it," he shouted. "You don't even know when your friend is in danger. You're all so apathetic about real trouble right in front of you."

With his anger escalating, Marisa wanted to get away from him as quickly as possible.

"Look, Dustin, I said I would talk to her. What more do you think I can do?"

He grabbed her by the arm. "Take it seriously! Act like you believe she's in danger! As a matter of fact, you are all probably in danger. She showed me the list, Marisa. I think it's Coach Rob who wrote it in the first place."

"That's crazy, Dustin." She shook loose from his grasp. "You really need to leave." But he didn't move. "Go! Before I get my dad to come out here and make you go!" Marisa shouted.

"You'll be so sorry," Dustin told her. "You three have no idea."

Marisa was shaking by the time Dustin got in his car. *Something is wrong with him*, Marisa thought, jumping on the Dustin-is-a-lunatic bandwagon.

"*Mi hija*, who was that guy?" her mother asked when she walked into the house.

"It's probably her new boyfriend," her little sister Isi teased.

"That was not my boyfriend, and I don't want any of you talking to him if he comes back around. Okay?"

She went to her room. She was not comfortable with the fact that he had just showed up at her house, and *really* not comfortable with the fact that he could become so irate so quickly. She was more afraid of Shane being around *him* than Coach Rob. *I see what Brandi means about him. Maybe he is a crazy stalker.*

CHAPTER 16

Help Wanted

By the end of spring break, the girls' belief that Dustin was the person behind the list had now become fact. The weekend was the only thing that stood between them and the rest of the school year.

"I can't believe that he showed up at your house, Mari," Shane told her. "I'm still in shock about that."

"Yeah, well, we can't wait any longer. May first gets closer and closer every day," Brandi told them.

"We have to tell Mrs. Montgomery." Marisa was adamant.

"Okay, okay. I'll tell her," Shane said. "What will Dustin say when he's pulled into that office, though?" she continued. "There's no telling." She was afraid of him outing her relationship, but the thought of there being a doomsday was beyond her imagination.

"Now, let's get to that beach party. I'm ready to show off my bikini bottom," Brandi told them.

"Okay, SpongeBob!"

"More like Sandy. Don't nobody better say nothing about Texas!"

"You dumb!" Shane said, popping her with her towel.

They loaded up their cooler and headed off. The cabin they were going to was forty-five minutes away. There was a party being thrown by Ella Pearson. Marisa had met her at the very first Gap audition.

Ella had achieved a lot of success in her modeling career since then. Her photos were in some of the hottest teen magazines in the country. She and Marisa kept in touch over Friender. They had so much common. Marisa had confided in her about everything that was going on with the list.

"Girl, that's way too serious for me. Y'all need to come to my beach party and let your hair down. Put all that Port City drama behind you."

Ella had been right. The year had already been heavy enough when they lost Bethany, and now this. It was time for some fun.

They jumped out of the Jeep that Marisa had rented for their trip and went straight into the cabin. When they walked in, there was barely room to move. There was a little bit of everything for everyone's taste: pretty boys, rich boys, gym rats, older guys, younger guys, dark skin, light skin. Heaven.

The girls were plentiful too, and the collection of swimsuits was amazing. Model girls loved fashion, and it was obvious that this group was the up-and-coming in the Texas modeling business. If you studied fashion the way they did, some models were even recognizable.

Marisa searched for Ella, but they were hard-pressed to find her. They went to get drinks out of the coolers and started to mingle with the guests. There was a lot of flirting going on, and they were enjoying the easy freedom that being at the beach brought.

When they found Ella, she was playing drinking games with her guests. "Marisa!" she yelled, seeing her Friender friend in person for the first time in over a year. "I'm so glad you're here." She was slurring her words, but she knew it. "I'm losing," she told them.

"This is Shane and Brandi."

"I feel like I already know you two,

but nice to meet you. Are you staying the night? Did you find a room to crash? This place has like ten bedrooms."

"Yeah, we are definitely staying," Shane told Ella. "This is my kinda party."

"Ooh, a kindred spirit," Ella said, putting her arm through Shane's. "Come on, let me introduce y'all to some of my people."

Even a little tipsy, Ella was very beautiful. It was obvious why her career was taking off. She definitely had the wow factor, but she was also a party animal. Ella kept them up all night. When she had an idea to start a bonfire, she made all the guys round up wood on the beach. They roasted marshmallows, sang songs, and stayed up until dawn just enjoying the moonlit sky and cool sea breeze.

After watching the sunrise over the water, they decided it was time to get a little sleep before getting on the highway back to Port City. There was a huge couch in the living room where the three of them wound up sleeping. They figured if they stayed together, they would be safe. That was their only rule, especially after all the partying that this group had done.

Before they got on the road, they thanked Ella for a great night, grabbed breakfast at the local IHOP, and hit the highway back to Port City and back to the drama they had escaped, even if it was only for one night.

On Monday morning, they started the first round of testing for the state examinations. Shane could barely stay focused. She should have talked to Mrs. Montgomery before she sat down to take the test. Maybe then she could have focused better. When she was done, she raised her hand to get Mrs. Smith's attention.

"Are you done, Shane?" Mrs. Smith asked after she had motioned for Shane to approach her desk.

"Yes, ma'am. Do you mind writing me a pass to speak to Mrs. Montgomery?"

"Not today, Shane. She's extremely busy with testing."

"If I wait until after testing, it may be too late."

Mrs. Smith saw the urgency on her face. "Is everything okay, Shane?"

"Not really," she admitted, but she was not about to have Mrs. Smith all up in her business.

After Shane received the pass, she wondered if she should go and talk to Coach Rob first, before telling the principal. She passed by his classroom, but another teacher was using his room to administer the test. She decided that it would not be wise to search for him. Too many people. Too many questions.

She headed straight for the office. She waited her turn to speak with Mrs. Montgomery. She clutched the note tightly in her hands, to the point that she marked her palms with impressions of her finger-nails. "Shane Foster," the secretary said

She walked to the back where the principal was and slumped down in the chair in front of her desk.

"Hi, Shane. My staff said it was urgent that you see me, but they also said that you refused to tell them why."

"I think I can show you better than I can tell you." She handed the note over to Mrs. Montgomery. Shane watched as her face went from pleasant to fully shocked and then worried. It made Shane a little nervous too. *How serious is this?*

"Shane, where did you get this?"

"Some girl gave it to me in the auditorium the day of the assembly."

The principal swallowed hard. "You've had this all this time?"

"Yes, ma'am."

"Why, Shane? Why didn't you tell me sooner?" Her voice was full of concern, but Shane just felt as though she was in

the hot seat. It was one of the many questions that she preferred not to answer.
She started talking, explaining. Maybe too
much.

"Could you identify the girl who gave it
to you?" Mrs. Montgomery asked.

"I don't think so. I barely looked at her.
I'd never met her before."

"Well, hopefully we have the tape from
that day. Don't worry, Shane. I'm going to
get to the bottom of this. Who else knows
about the list?"

"Brandi and Marisa. Oh, and Dustin
Chaisson." The words slipped out of her
mouth. She wanted to jump out and catch
them, but it was too late. Her intention
was *not* to direct them to Dustin. He was
the only person who could incriminate
Coach Rob.

"Brandi Haywood, Marisa Maldonado, and Dustin Chaisson," Mrs. Montgomery repeated. "Okay, let me work on
this. I'll probably be calling you back in

here. I really wish you would have come to me earlier, Shane." The principal took a deep breath, as if this were the last thing she needed to happen at PCH. "Now, just focus on testing this week. I'll worry about this, okay?"

Shane agreed and headed back to class. She still had to tell Coach Rob before Mrs. Montgomery did, but that article Dustin gave her made her want to stay away from him.

CHAPTER 17

Doomsday

$\mathcal{E}$ach one of the people on the list was called into Mrs. Montgomery's office so they could be officially notified that they could be in danger. Marisa, Shane, and Brandi had known about it for so long that the threat had lost its sting. When Mrs. Montgomery informed them that they would be allowed to miss school on May first, each of them declined.

"I'm not going to start running now, Mrs. Montgomery. I'm a fighter," Brandi told her. Mrs. Montgomery shook her head. That was one fact nobody could argue with. Brandi Haywood had faced adversity and won.

"We already talked about this, Mrs. Montgomery. I'll be here too," Shane notified her.

"And I'm with them," Marisa said, sighing deeply. She was just relieved that an adult knew about the list. Surprisingly, nobody told Mrs. Montgomery about Shane and Coach Rob. Shane was like a cat. She always seemed to land on her feet.

Mrs. Monroe had not been told about the list until she was called into the office a week before D-Day. She had never been threatened before. For the most part, her students liked her. She couldn't understand why anyone would want to harm her or the other people on the list.

By the time she left Mrs. Montgomery's office, school was over. She was relieved, because she was in tears and didn't want her students to see her upset. She sat at her desk, staring out of the window. Her husband had told her to get a corporate job instead of teaching, but she loved shaping young minds. No matter how dangerous schools across the country were becoming, she couldn't leave. Now she had to go home and tell him that her name had appeared on a hit list. The thought of having that conversation made her cry even more.

"Mrs. Monroe," Shane said as she entered the classroom. Mrs. Monroe grabbed tissues from her desk to try and wipe away her tears, but she was too late. "Are you okay?" Shane felt so bad. She knew why her favorite teacher was crying.

"I'm okay, Shane. Are you okay?"

"Yes, ma'am. I had a little more time to process it all. I was the one who received the letter in the first place."

"I don't know why I'm so upset. It was probably just a silly prank."

"Yeah, I think so. Are you coming to school that day?"

"I don't know, Shane. I'm going to have to think about that one. You may want to discuss this with your parents. Were they notified?"

"I don't know." She had never thought about the school notifying her parents. That was the last thing she wanted. Her plan was to get through the first day of May alive and then ... well, she'd figure the rest out after that. She felt a little sad when she left Mrs. Monroe. She hated to see her so upset.

Nobody talked about the list much that week, but when May first finally arrived, TV crews were in the parking lot. There were also a lot of police cars. One officer was doing an interview with a reporter from Channel 11.

It was like driving up to a totally different school. Nothing felt normal. The girls immediately tensed up, sitting in the student parking lot looking out at the chaos. The officers were trying to get students off the buses and into the school.

"Do you think we should be here?" Marisa asked nervously. "I mean, Mrs. Montgomery said we could stay home."

"I'm staying at school," Shane said, getting out of the car abruptly. "I understand if you two want to leave."

"I don't know. I mean ... our names were actually on the list," Brandi said, taking Marisa's side. "You sure about this, Shane?"

"Well, I think we are all going to be okay," Shane replied. "It was just a stupid prank."

"That's yo' white side talking," Brandi shot back. "Like in the movies, always wanting to go and check on the sound in the basement. 'Hello? Hello? Anybody down there?' And then *bam*!"

"The black people always die first, so stop."

"That's my point," replied Brandi. "My

black behind don't need to follow your lead on this one. Shoot, I'll be collateral damage."

"You two are certifiable," Marisa said, rolling her eyes. "This is no time for jokes. Are we going in or not?"

"I'm going," Shane announced. Brandi and Marisa reluctantly followed her lead. They also got out of the car. When they walked into the school, they were stopped at the door by a female police officer with a metal detector. "You ladies need to open your purses and backpacks, then step to the side so they can check you."

The girls looked nervously at one another. It was feeling less and less like a prank. "Can you hear my heart?" Marisa asked Brandi.

"No, can you hear mine?"

Marisa just shook her head no.

Shane shook her head at both of them. "Y'all should have gone to Starbucks or something."

"Once you come in, you will not be allowed back out," the officer informed them.

The atmosphere was more intense than they had imagined. The teachers seemed melancholy in the classrooms. Everything had a serious tone: their assignments, the lectures, everything. When Shane arrived at her journalism class, she was not surprised to see a substitute teacher sitting in Mrs. Monroe's chair. She didn't think that Mrs. Monroe would come to school.

During fifth period, everyone was startled when fire alarms started to go off. You could tell by the teachers' faces that they were scared too. It was obvious that this was not a planned drill. The teachers tried to put on a brave face for the kids, but students had a sixth sense when it came to their teachers. They could tell that something was amiss.

Some kids said that a teacher screamed when the alarms sounded. As they left their classrooms, it was obvious that the threat was being taken seriously. There was no playing or joking. There was dead silence as everyone left the building.

Students weren't just gossiping about screaming teachers. Rumor had it that there was a bomb threat. That's why the firm alarm sounded. After about an hour of waiting, the students were restless. The sun was beating down on them. They asked to call their parents. The list was spooking the entire student body. Nobody knew what to expect next.

Shane noticed Coach Rob with a group of students and went over to talk to him. "Hey, can I talk to you for a second?"

"Not here, Shane."

"Then where? It's kind of important."

She knew Coach didn't know what the big emergency could be. She had been brushing him off for nearly six weeks. He told Shane to follow him, and he led her through the crowd.

"Coach Reynolds, I could use your assistance with this group of students," Assistant Principal Spears informed him.

"Yes, sir. Let me finish up with this student. I'll be right back."

He opened an outside door leading to his office. "What is so urgent, Shane? There are much more pressing matters than your feelings about me right now."

"Whoa, cool down. I just wanted to show you something." She dug in her bag and pulled out the article. She knew it would get him. But when she handed it to him, he didn't even flinch.

"And? Is this it, Shane? Because I have a job to do."

"Is this it? Really, Rob? Is that you?"

"It's my name, isn't it? That was an incident that I don't like talking about, and I shouldn't have to explain myself to you."

"Don't and watch what I do," Shane threatened him, knowing that she would never turn him in. She wasn't like that.

"Look, I was framed by a teenager and her aunt. I was involved with the girl's aunt. I admit it, I cheated on her, but not with her niece, with another woman. She found out about it, and she pulled out all the stops to frame me.

"There was no evidence against me" continued Coach Rob. "If there had been any, I wouldn't have been hired here at Port City High."

Shane was so relieved. She could feel her attitude toward him changing instantly. She hugged him tightly. "I knew it. I knew you weren't a monster."

"Is that why you haven't been coming to see me?" he asked, pulling away from her.

Before she could answer, the bomb squad entered his office.

"Nobody should be in this building, sir. How did you get in?"

"It's my office."

"You been in here this whole time?"

"No, sir. I just walked in. Why am I being questioned?"

"We have reason to believe the bomb threat came from this office."

"This office? That's crazy." Coach Rob started to look nervous.

"Sir, who has access to your office?"

"Nobody." There was a faraway gaze on Coach's face.

"Sir?" the officer asked. "Is there something we should know?"

Shane studied Coach Rob. She knew he was trying to keep a secret, but this was too serious. "Um ... yes, a student asked to type her essay in my office, Kylie ... Kylie Manuel." He avoided Shane's gaze, which was piercing his soul.

"And what about this young lady here? What is your name, miss?"

"Shane Foster, but I walked in with Coach Rob ... I mean Coach Reynolds."

The officer looked at her suspiciously. "Last name is Foster?"

Shane swallowed hard. She didn't want him to make the connection to her father. "Um ... yes. Is there anything else, or can I go?"

Just as Shane was turning to leave his office through the side door, another officer was walking in with Kylie. When Kylie saw Shane, she lost it. "I knew it! You told me you didn't want anything to do with her, Rob! Liar!" She spat in his face. He nervously wiped his cheek.

The officer who was originally speaking with Coach Reynolds looked at him in disbelief. "Do we need to talk about this at the station?"

"No, sir. This girl is deranged. I have no idea what she's talking about. I'm starting to think she did have something to do with all of this chaos." Coach seemingly would say anything to throw the officer off track.

"Yeah, and I'm starting to think the baby I'm carrying is yours," Kylie retorted.

You could hear a pin drop. Then everyone gasped. Shane stepped back to distance herself from Coach Rob, but tripped over a chair behind her.

"Oh my ..." She grabbed her throat. Kylie? Pregnant? With Coach Rob's baby! It was too much.

"She's lying! I never laid a hand on her!"

"Oh, you did more than that, Coach," Kylie said, her eyes smoldering. She turned to the officer. "I'm telling the truth."

"Well, since you're telling the truth, young lady ... did you call in the bomb threat?" The officer saw an opening and jumped on it. Kylie was talking, and he had to keep her talking.

"I did! I had to. He left me no choice."

"What do you mean? Why did he leave you no choice?" the officer asked.

"Shut up, Kylie! Seriously," Coach Rob told her.

"Take him out of here." Once Coach Reynolds was escorted from his office,

Kylie broke down. Shane wished they would have escorted her out too, but she was left there to witness the whole sordid story.

"Coach Rob and I are a couple. Well, were. We have been together since the beginning of the school year. He told me that this skank was coming on to him," she said, pointing at Shane. "And he said that if I wasn't careful, I could be replaced."

Shane nervously looked at the officers. "He lied to you, Kylie. I'm not involved in this at all."

"Shane, you have to tell someone if he made advances," the officer told her. "These are serious accusations."

"I'm a big girl. I'm well aware of the seriousness of the accusations. But it sounds like Kylie's carrying all the proof you need in her belly." Shane started to walk out of the office. She was not needed here.

"Last question, Kylie," the officer asked. "Did you send that list out?"

"What list?" she asked smugly.

That's when Shane stopped in her tracks. She hadn't put two and two together yet. "You did it, didn't you, Kylie? You've turned my life upside down. It was you! You stankin' ..." Shane lunged for her.

"You deserved it, Miss Perfect!" Kylie shouted. "It was good to see you and your little friends squirm. Teacher's pet. Coach's pet. Everyone loves Shane Foster. And whoever loves you got listed. Forget you and them!"

Shane finally got close enough to Kylie. She slapped her across the face. "If you weren't pregnant, I'd beat the living—"

Kylie was shocked. "I'm pressing charges. You psycho broad!"

"No, ma'am. *We* are pressing charges," the officer said, putting handcuffs on her.

"Stop it. I'm pregnant. You're going to hurt my baby!" Kylie shrieked.

"We won't, miss." He led her out of Coach Rob's office, past the students still outside, and into a patrol car. Shane followed them to the front of the building where she saw Brandi and Marisa. They ran over to her and hugged her tightly. Kylie stared at them with hatred from the patrol car.

Coach Rob was next. He was escorted out of the main building by another officer. He had to walk past students and faculty. He was put into the patrol car next to Kylie's. Principal Montgomery followed close behind, ensuring that he was off of her campus.

Another coach announced on a bull-horn, "Teachers, you can escort your students back to class at this time. The threat is over."

Everyone slowly moved back into the building. Shane, Brandi, and Marisa stayed behind, watching as the patrol cars pulled away from the school with Kylie and Coach Rob.

Mrs. Montgomery walked over to them. "I'm going to call your parents. You girls should go home. You've been through a lot today. Come by my office so I can sign you out. You are to go straight home. I want a phone call from each of you confirming that you are safe and sound."

They each nodded, relieved that this ordeal was behind them.

CHAPTER 18

Shane

The first person they saw when they walked out of the office was Dustin Chaisson. They looked at each other, remembering everything they had accused him of doing. All along, he had been in the same boat with them. Kylie's hit list had wrecked their trust in him.

Dustin had the unfortunate task of trying to clear his name and not freak out, all at the same time. What was there to say when someone had been wrongfully accused? Sometimes sorry just doesn't seem like enough.

Shane felt the most to blame. "Hey, Dustin."

"Hey, Shane. I'm just waiting for the principal to sign me out. Everyone whose name was on the list or knew about the list from the beginning is getting to go home now."

"Yeah, that's why we're here. We just got signed out." She paused, trying to find her words. "Dustin, I'm sorry that I ever thought—"

"Hey, it's okay."

"I should be the one apologizing," Brandi said, interrupting their conversation. "I'm more to blame than Shane. I convinced them both that ..." Her voice trailed off. It was always hard admitting fault. Dustin was silent, which made it even more difficult. He scrolled through his phone as if she wasn't even talking.

"Dustin, please. I know that you're new to Port City, and I'm not trying to make any excuses ... but I've been through a lot.

I'm suspicious of people. If you can find it in your heart to forgive me—"

"It's good, Brandi." He cut her off. "We were all just looking out for Shane. I had a bad feeling about that guy, and then when I found out about his past, I kinda lost it." He took a deep breath. "I guess I should be apologizing to you too." He looked up for the first time during their conversation.

"Thanks," Brandi said, smiling at him.

"Now, speaking of the past," Shane interrupted them, coughing into her hand. "What's up with the mug shot?" Brandi and Marisa giggled uncomfortably. It was typical Shane not to worry about timing.

He stared down the hallway. The day of that mug shot, his whole life had changed. "I don't like to talk about it."

"Hey, we are way past that. Spill it," Shane told him.

He seemed to be searching his brain for the right words. "That was the day I found out that my little sister's babysitter had been the cause of the bruises on her body. When I went to the house to confront her, I kinda lost it."

"Yeah, you tend to do that," Brandi said, getting elbowed by Marisa. "What? He does."

"I know ... I know. I have a temper. But it's worse when it involves people I care about." Shane started to smile when he looked in her direction. He was talking about his sister, but she knew that he meant her too.

"Look, I came to Port City to start fresh. That wasn't something I wanted to bring here with me." He showed them Madison's picture.

"Ah, she's adorable," Marisa said. "She reminds me of you, Shane, when you were younger."

"Yeah, I guess that's why I was so protective," Dustin said.

The principal's secretary came through the door. "Okay, we've contacted your parents, and they said you are free to go. They wanted to come and pick you up, but Mrs. Montgomery said that you were going to leave together. Dustin, your mom is at work. One of the officers can take you home."

"No, I'll take him home," Brandi jumped in. They walked the long hallway to the students' parking lot. "Jerry's?" Brandi asked before unlocking the car doors.

"Girl, we told Mrs. Montgomery we'd go right home. But Jerry's sounds way better to me. I'm in," Shane said, smiling at the people she cared about the most, even Dustin.

CHAPTER 19

Marisa

*I*t was the night of the play. Marisa nervously put the finishing touches on her costume. As she looked in the mirror, she could barely see any scars on her face. Dr. Neimann had truly delivered on his promises. There was only one round of treatment left, which would be done over the summer. Finally, she would be able to put the whole accident behind her.

Her final photo shoot for the plastic surgery center was scheduled to take place in Houston shortly after her last treatment. Only one more trip to Cali. By the beginning of her senior year, she was sure she wouldn't even need makeup anymore.

One thing that the accident did teach her about was inner beauty. When she felt that her outside appearance had been permanently altered, she had to look within herself to find out who she truly was. That's when she discovered dancing. Now, she was about to share that newfound love with her community.

She had already performed the part of Tania flawlessly. When Tania lost her mother, the audience held their breath. The first act went off without a hitch. It was moving, touching, and riveting.

Everything was fast-paced backstage. Marisa had changed into her costume for her monologue. This upcoming scene made her the most nervous. The muscles in her legs shook and throbbed as she tried to get them back under her control. When she danced her way onto the stage, the crowd gave a small cheer.

She could hear her parents. She could hear Shane and Brandi. She could feel their support. It made her nervousness dissipate. She was in the moment, telling her character's story. In that moment, she was Tania. When the scene was over, there was no doubt in anyone's mind that her body had been created to dance. She could hear the crowd cheering as she left the stage. It was magical. The drama team had worked hard, and it showed.

After the play was over, they introduced the student performers, calling them to the stage. Mr. Maldonado was next to the stairs with a bouquet of roses for Marisa. He looked at his daughter and simply nodded, handing her the flowers. Then he kissed her cheek and quickly exited the stage.

"What a night!" she exclaimed later as she joined her friends and family.

"It's not over yet, mi hija. We have to go out to celebrate."

Her sisters and brother hugged her tightly. Isi tried to imitate her sister's dance moves, and Nadia tried to stop Isi. "She's so embarrassing," Nadia said.

"Oh, let her be," Marisa told Nadia softly. "She'll have time to be serious later."

They decided on a traditional Southeast Texas meal of all-you-can-eat barbeque crabs, shrimp, and gumbo.

Marisa sat next to her mother during the dinner. "You looked absolutely beautiful tonight, mi hija."

"Thank you. The scarring is almost gone."

"Oh, I'm not talking about your face. I meant the beauty from the inside. You shined out there. You could have done that with or without plastic surgery."

"I know, Mama. I felt it too. I think I found myself, ya know?"

"I do. And I love who you are." She wrapped her arm around her daughter and squeezed her tightly.

CHAPTER 20

Brandi

The debate team was still in the statewide tournament. They were considered tough competitors, but the upcoming opponents from Dallas were one of the best groups in Texas. In this debate the PCH team would be arguing in support of the death penalty. They were thoroughly prepared.

When Brandi spoke for the team, she delivered. She was in her element. Erick had done the closing remarks for their team. His argument was skillfully crafted and flawlessly executed. He was a true contender.

Their victory over the Dallas team had earned them a place at the state finals in the capital of Austin. It was an honor to compete at the state finals. Winning would come with a lot of attention and acclaim.

"I'm not arguing at state," Brandi told Erick when he said he wanted her by his side for the final debate of his high school career. "Let one of our other teammates do it, Erick. I'll be too nervous. You have too much riding on it."

"We're all nervous, Brandi. You'll do fine. I think you are underestimating how much this team relies on you. You're smart, talented, and beautiful. It's a winning combination."

"Beautiful, eh," she said as she moved her eyebrows up and down.

"Girl, you know you're beautiful. I didn't mean it like that." Erick had never crossed the line with her, not even in the slightest. They had formed a true friend-ship and Brandi loved it. She'd never had a successful relationship. She could be too much for most guys. Or she just picked the wrong one. Over and over again. Besides, those three qualities Erick admired could be intimidating. Erick saw her beauty and wanted to preserve it, not put her on display as a selfish act. He was truly a good guy.

Brandi's parents decided to accompany her on the trip to Austin. Raven had bugged them to join. She wanted to watch her big sister compete. "Raven, Brandi's going to be debating immigration reform. You won't even know what they are talking about," her mother said.

"I will too," Raven protested. "When Brandi breaks down a topic, I always get it. She talks on my level."

"Well, if RaRa gets it, I know I'm doing my job. I like to simplify topics."

"Hm, I have to admit," her dad said, "you do a great job of that. That's it! We are going to Austin. I'm going to see my baby compete. Cat, make sure you take off that weekend. That hospital has been working you too much anyway."

"I can't argue with that. We'll make it a Haywood road trip!"

When they arrived in Austin, Brandi fell in love. *I like it here*, she thought. As soon as they put their bags down, they left to find the barbeque place that they had seen advertised on a Texas travel channel. It was located on the Sixth Street strip. They were able to listen to live music while dining on the patio. The Haywood family looked happy, and they truly were.

By the next day, Brandi's nerves were shot. It was competition time. She met up with Erick and the rest of the team to iron out the details of the debate.

When they came face-to-face with the opposing team from Katy, Texas, each group of students eyed the other.

Erick stood up. The other team's captain approached the PCH group. "Good luck today," he said, extending his hand.

"Good luck to y'all too," Erick replied.

Erick and Brandi were a two-person team, and the way they delivered the information brought the house down. The debate was exciting and timely. By the time Brandi began to tell Marisa's family story about their struggles for citizenship, they knew they were winning the debate. The audience could feel the urgency. But it was Erick's closing argument, which focused on human rights, that brought the people to their feet. He had done what he set out to do, and Brandi was happy to be along for the ride.

When Port City High School was announced the winner of the debate, earning the title of state champions, Brandi and Erick joined their team and families sitting in the audience. It was time to celebrate.

They were interrupted by a scout from the University of Texas, who was interested in recruiting them to attend the school. The proposition of a scholarship for doing what they loved was cause for even more celebration and happiness.

Before leaving Austin, the Haywood family decided to stop and speak to the UT scout one more time. He gave them a tour of the university and talked to them at length about the possibilities for Brandi's future. "I have another year of school to complete," she told him.

"Yes, we are aware of that," he said, laughing. "But when the time is right, we would love for you to begin the next phase of your life here at UT."

A smile slowly crept to Brandi's face. "I guess there's only one thing to say: hook 'em horns," she said, putting her fingers in the traditional University of Texas hand signal. Brandi had found where she belonged for the next four years after she completed high school. *If* she scored well on her SATs. *And* if she kept her grades up.

The best part was that she wouldn't have to do it alone. Erick would be there for a whole year before her. He would be able to show her the ropes when she arrived. Before she got back in the car, she looked back at the university. *I'll be back.* She smiled as she looked at her future home.

Epilogue

The last day of school always had an emotional vibe. The senior class wasn't there because graduation was scheduled for that night. The junior class was in limbo, as they were not officially seniors yet. But they were definitely the big dogs on campus. By lunchtime, the whole junior class decided that their school day was officially over. They left PCH to the freshman and sophomores and headed to the bowling alley.

As the girls laced up their shoes, they

looked at each other and laughed. Here they were, another school year behind them, and their senior year so close they could taste it. After all they had been through during the year, they were excited for a fresh start. Only a new school year could bring that.

"Are you thinking what I'm thinking?" Shane asked her friends.

"Nobody is ever thinking what you are thinking, Shane," Marisa said.

"Do tell, my BFF. What's going through that pretty little mind of yours?" Brandi asked.

"I'm thinking that we are going to beat the pants off Ashley and her friends. We should have done this a long time ago." They had been at odds with Ashley and her friends for forever, but the closer they got to graduation, the easier it was to put all that animosity behind them. Since twirling together, Ashley and Marisa had come to the point where they could peacefully coexist.

"We can hear you, Shane," Ashley said as she put the names into the computer.

"I know," Shane snorted, and it was a wonderful sound to her friends. She had been way too serious this year. Her relationship with Coach Rob had sent her in a negative spiral, though Shane was not going to admit it.

After the list came out, she was finally forced to look at her actions and how they were affecting not only her, but the people around her.

Although they had all been through a lot, they had come through transformed. Like a butterfly's metamorphosis from a caterpillar. Each girl was beautiful and fully formed. Different colors. Different personalities. Different shapes. With the self-confidence they could only dream about a year ago.

And they were determined that their senior year would be their best year ever. With summer break only hours away, it was time to leave the past in the past and get ready for some fun. After all, that's what high school was all about.

ABOUT THE AUTHOR

Shannon Freeman

*B*orn and raised in Port Arthur, Texas, Shannon Freeman works full time as an English teacher in her hometown. After completing college at Oral Roberts University, Freeman began her work in the classroom teaching English and oral communications. At that time, the characters of her breakout series, Port City High, began to form, but these characters would not come to life for years. An apartment fire destroyed almost all of the young teacher's worldly possessions before she could begin writing. With nothing to lose, Freeman packed up and headed to Los Angeles, California, to pursue a passion that burned within her since her youth, the entertainment industry.

Beginning in 2001, Freeman made numerous television appearances and enjoyed a rich life full of friends and hard work. In 2008, her world once again changed when she and her husband, Derrick Freeman, found out that they were expecting their first child. Freeman then made the difficult decision to return to Port Arthur and start the family that she had always wanted.

At that time, Freeman returned to the classroom, but entertaining others was still a desire that could not be quenched. Being in the classroom again inspired her to tell the story of Marisa, Shane, and

Brandi that had been evolving for almost a decade. She began to write and the Port City High series was born.

Port City High is the culmination of Freeman's life experiences, including her travels across the United States and Europe. Her stories reflect the friendships she's made across the globe. Port City High is the next breakout series for today's young adult readers. Freeman says, "The topics are relevant and life changing. I just hope that people are touched by my characters' stories as much as I am."